"You seri̶̶̶̶̶̶ I'd allow you to make love to me?" Olivia demanded hoarsely.

Adam's eyes glinted with dark fire. "Oh, I wasn't thinking of asking permission," he murmured. "Not that I think you'd refuse."

"Why, you arrogant..." Without even forming the conscious intention of hitting him, she swung her hand to his face.

He caught it swiftly in midair, his fingers closing around hers like a vice. "Am I?" He drew her hand up to his lips, laying one scalding kiss against the tumultuous pulse inside her wrist, sending a shimmer of heat right through her. "But you know that I'm right, don't you, my lovely, desirable Angel? There's a certain inevitability about it—there always has been."

SUSANNE McCARTHY grew up in South London but she always wanted to live in the country, and shortly after her marriage she moved to Shropshire with her husband. They live in a house on a hill with lots of dogs and cats. She loves to travel—but she loves to come home. As well as her writing, she still enjoys her career as a teacher in adult education, though she only works part-time now.

Books by Susanne McCarthy

SUSANNE McCARTHY

A Candle For The Devil

Harlequin Books

TORONTO • NEW YORK • LONDON
AMSTERDAM • PARIS • SYDNEY • HAMBURG
STOCKHOLM • ATHENS • TOKYO • MILAN
MADRID • WARSAW • BUDAPEST • AUCKLAND

ISBN 0-373-11748-5

A CANDLE FOR THE DEVIL

Copyright © 1991 by Susanne McCarthy.

First North American Publication 1995.

Printed in U.S.A.

CHAPTER ONE

'WELL, of all the nerve!'

Eleanor Lambert, newly widowed and formidably elegant in just the right degree of mourning, could stop a charging rhinoceros in its tracks with that glare. Olivia glanced over her shoulder to see who had incurred her stepmother's displeasure, and froze.

'Oh, my goodness,' she breathed. 'What on earth is *he* doing here? It's been years!'

'I should think it's pretty obvious what he's doing here,' Eleanor snorted. 'He's here to cause trouble. He could at least have waited until after the funeral! But I suppose it's only to be expected.'

For one awful moment, Olivia thought she was going to faint. Fortunately, if anyone noticed her pallor they would put it down to the occasion. Cautiously she risked another covert look across the room. There was quite a crowd of people assembled in the drawing-room—the firm of Lambert, Taylor & Simpson was a major employer in the region, and everyone wished to pay their last respects to the man who had been its founder and driving force for the past fifty years.

Adam Taylor was perfectly well aware of the disturbance his presence had caused, but he was acting as if he was totally oblivious to it all. The arrogant set of his wide shoulders warned that the past six years had done nothing to change him. That hard-boned face was perhaps a little leaner now, but his hair was as thick and dark as ever, and he still had that indefinable aura of masculine power that was so fatally attractive to women.

As if he sensed her watching him, he turned, and his eyes caught hers—and she felt as if her heartbeat had slowed to a halt. He acknowledged her with a cynical twist of a smile, and she returned a glare of undisguised contempt, ignoring the calculated way he turned to smile down at the woman at his side.

Trust Georgina, Olivia reflected tartly. Anything to shock, as her appearance today testified. She had chosen to wear a cherry-red suit that glowed like a rude word at a vicarage tea-party. Her make-up had been applied with the hand of Dracula, and her harshly bleached blonde hair looked as if it had been styled with an egg-whisk.

The sheer bad taste of bringing Adam to Lex's funeral had probably appealed to her. Besides, she had always fancied him—she had made that embarrassingly clear, even when she had been married to someone else. It was strange that Eleanor's niece, Richard's sister, should be so different from the rest of the family...

Richard had come to her side. 'Have you seen who's here?' he asked quietly, resting a proprietorial hand on her waist.

'Yes.' Somehow she managed to force a smile. 'I suppose it was inevitable that he would show up sooner or later.'

'He might have had the decency to wait for at least a few days!' he grated, unconsciously echoing his aunt's words. 'Well, if he's expecting to walk back into the company and start throwing his weight around, he can just think again. He only holds one third of the shares. Even if Georgie's fool enough to support him—which she probably is—he'll still only be able to muster forty-three per cent—his thirty-three and her ten. You and I together can block him every time.'

'Perhaps he's come to offer to let us buy him out?' mused Olivia doubtfully. 'With Lex gone, the proxy expires...'

Richard laughed drily. 'I'd like to think so. I resent the fact that we do all the work, and he sits back sunning himself in Australia, taking a third of our profits for doing nothing at all.'

'Do please try to avoid a scene,' put in his aunt, her concern for the proprieties uppermost in her mind, as usual.

'Don't worry, Eleanor,' Richard assured her grimly. 'If there's to be a scene, it won't be of my making.'

'Perhaps we should circulate?' suggested Eleanor. 'I think it would be best if we all behaved as if nothing had happened.'

It took all of Olivia's iron-trained self-discipline to move around the room, pretending not to hear the whispers. It had been a long time—six years— but no one around here would have forgotten. Nervously she fingered the large diamond ring on her left hand—Richard's ring. Six years ago it had been Adam's ring she had been wearing. She had taken it off, and hidden it away in a dark corner of her dressing-table drawer, the day he was arrested...

'Such a terribly sad loss for you. He'll be missed by us all. Still, I suppose he'd had quite a good innings—seventy-two years old. And these last few years...'

'Yes—thank you.' She was murmuring all the conventional responses to the conventional expressions of sympathy, but she was aware that Adam was just behind her. She couldn't simply ignore him completely, however much she would have preferred to do so. That would cause even more comment.

She had managed to compose herself rather well, though her heart gave a nervous little thump as she turned and found him closer to her than she had expected. She was tall in her neat-heeled court shoes, but she had to look up at him. The custom-tailored elegance of his grey suit did nothing to disguise the hard, muscular maleness of his body, and there was no mistaking the cold hostility beneath that urbane façade.

'Good afternoon, Adam,' she managed, offering him her hand in formal greeting.

He let his eyes drift down over her in a cool appraisal, registering an insolent approval of her slender figure in the trim black suit. 'Hi, Angel,' he responded laconically.

A shimmer of heat ran through her; he had always called her Angel... Bravely she struggled for some semblance of composure, determined not to let him see that he had the least effect on her. 'I'm glad you could come.'

He lifted one cynical eyebrow. 'Are you?' he enquired, a mocking note in his voice.

He had ignored her hand, and she let it drop to her side, a slight tinge of pink colouring her cheeks as she sought desperately for something else to say. 'It ... It's been a long time.'

'It has indeed.'

'You're ... still living in Sydney?' An unpleasant dizziness was swirling around her head, and her voice sounded unsteady even to her own ears. She was aware that the rest of the family were closing ranks behind her—Richard, and Eleanor, and Richard's mother, Frances Simpson.

'What are you doing here, Taylor?' Richard demanded, none of Olivia's pretended politeness in his voice.

Those dark eyes glinted with a sardonic humour. 'Why, the same as everybody else,' he drawled. 'I've come to pay my last respects to Lex.'

'You're not welcome in this house,' Eleanor informed him sharply.

He looked at her, a look that would have poisoned anyone less well-armoured than Eleanor. 'You made that clear enough six years ago,' he gibed, faintly menacing. 'You prevented me from seeing Lex.'

'Lex had no wish to see you,' she retorted with cold dignity. 'And why you should come here now ...!'

'I told you—I came for Lex's funeral.'

'Besides, he's with me,' put in Georgina, wrapping her hands possessively around his arm and challenging her family with her hard-faced defiance.

Her mother made a scornful noise. 'You never did have a grain of decency in you,' she snapped at her. 'Coming to a funeral dressed like that! I suppose you don't care what people think?'

'Not a fig!'

Adam lifted one eyebrow a fraction of an inch, glancing around the semi-circle of outraged faces with mocking contempt. 'What's wrong?' he enquired, a sardonic inflexion in his voice. 'Isn't *anyone* pleased to see me?'

Richard stepped forward to confront him, his shoulders square. 'If you've come to make trouble for the company, I might as well warn you that you're wasting your time,' he asserted. 'Between us, Olivia and I have the majority shareholding— there's nothing you can do to overturn any of our decisions.'

'Now why would I want to make trouble?' enquired Adam, the air of bland innocence a taunt in itself. 'I'm quite satisfied with the way the company's been run.'

'I'm sure you are.' Richard was betraying his anger. 'It's let you live the life of Riley these past six years...'

Those dark eyes became perceptibly harder. 'Not quite six years,' he reminded him, sinisterly quiet. 'For one year of it, if you remember, I was in prison. That wasn't exactly the life of Riley.'

Olivia felt as if she was choking, and no one else seemed able to speak. Adam favoured them all with a smile of cool derision, and moved away across the room, deliberately letting his hand slip down to rest over the pert curve of Georgina's derrière in the chic red suit.

Her mouth dry, Olivia reached for a glass of sherry from one of the maids Eleanor had hired in to lend a hand for the 'small gathering' after the funeral. She had forgotten—she had made herself forget—the way one look from those mesmerising dark eyes could make her heart flutter. Once she had been foolish enough to mistake that tug of physical attraction for love. Fortunately she had grown up since then.

Richard came to her side, putting a gentle hand on her arm. 'Are you all right, Olivia?' he enquired, his voice soft with concern.

'Oh . . . yes, I'm fine,' she assured him quickly. 'It was just rather a surprise, seeing him like that, after all this time.' She smiled up at him with warmth in her eyes. Dear Richard—he must be wondering. After all, she had been engaged to Adam before she had been engaged to him . . .

Three years, she accounted with a small jolt of surprise. Surely they hadn't intended it to be such a long engagement? But they'd been waiting for the right time, when the company could spare its chairman for long enough for him to take a honeymoon, and somehow things had just drifted.

'I'm afraid my dear sister has really excelled herself this time,' he remarked wryly, glancing across the room to where the other couple stood. 'Mother's simmering, and Eleanor's likely to slip arsenic in their sherry if they stay much longer.'

Olivia followed the direction of his gaze as Georgina's shrieking laugh sliced the dignified atmosphere—Adam had obviously said something funny. Her eyes were drawn inexorably to that dark head, just a little higher than the others around it.

'You know, I never did understand him, Richard,' she mused. 'Why did he do it? He had everything—he didn't need to resort to that kind of petty crime.'

Richard shrugged his shoulders. 'Maybe it all came too fast and too easy,' he suggested wisely. 'Stepping straight into his father's shoes when he was so young—Adam's the type who would have been better off if he'd had to carve a way for himself.'

'Yes... I suppose you're right.' Watching him now, even from this distance, she could sense that physical presence that caught the attention of everyone around him; when Adam Taylor was in a room, no one could ignore him. Had he found the prospect of running a large and established engineering company too dull? Had he needed another challenge so much that he had been prepared to risk everything for the excitement of pitting his wits against the police, as some men risked their lives in racing cars and other dangerous pursuits? Or had he thought he was above other men, too clever to get caught?

'It just bothers me what he might do,' Richard went on seriously. 'It wouldn't be in his best interests to do anything that might harm the company, but there's no guarantee that he'll behave rationally if he's come back looking for some sort of revenge.'

'Revenge?' She blinked at him in surprise. 'But why?' she protested. 'What happened to him was no one's fault but his own.'

Richard gave a wry smile. 'Who knows what goes on in a twisted mind like that?'

'What do you think he might do?' Olivia asked anxiously.

'I don't know. Hopefully he won't stay around very long—but until he leaves I think we should all be on our guard.'

As the afternoon wore on, Olivia found it increasingly hard to maintain her poise in front of all that throng of people. She hardly recognised the Lex she had known in the affectionate husband, doting father, benevolent employer everyone seemed to be talking about.

She had never been close to her father. The engineering company he had founded with his two friends, fifty years ago, had been his pride and his obsession. He had had little time for family life. Olivia had been a late baby, and her mother had died shortly after her birth.

He had married Eleanor, the sister-in-law of the third member of that triumvirate, as much for convenience as anything else—neither of them had ever made much secret of that. She kept his home running smoothly, and was the perfect hostess for his frequent business dinners; in return, she had enjoyed the wealth and status she considered her due.

In fact, if Lex had been fond of anyone, it was Adam. He had looked on him almost as the son he had never had, especially after Adam's own parents were killed in a car crash when he was just eighteen. It was Adam he had been grooming to take over from him as chairman of LTS in due course—until that awful day, six years ago.

No one in the company had suspected—well, they wouldn't, would they? He would hardly have advertised the fact that he was moonlighting as a common burglar. There had been a series of art thefts in the area—very professionally executed, according to the police. Whoever was behind them knew exactly what he was after, and must have had a ready market for them abroad; they were not the sort of items that could be re-sold through antiques shops and auction houses—they were too easily recognisable.

When a priceless fourteenth-century Chinese vase was found neatly packed in a crate of milling discs dispatched from one of the company's subsidiaries, the police had come round asking questions. There had been all sorts of rumours, of course; everyone had had their own theory. But Adam's arrest had come as a complete shock to everybody.

It had almost killed Lex. In his middle sixties, he had had all the health and vigour of a man twenty years younger; almost overnight he had been robbed of all that, turned into a frail old man. The last years of his life he had suffered a series of strokes, gradually deteriorating until he couldn't walk, couldn't use his right hand, couldn't hold a proper conversation.

The scandal had rocked the company to its foundations. With Lex in hospital, the confidence of customers had plunged and morale had been at rock bottom. It had chiefly been Richard who had hauled them through the crisis—even Lex had had to admit that he had done a good deal better than he had expected.

Richard had never minded that, even after what had happened, Lex should still be inclined to compare him unfavourably with Adam. 'He's old, and a little confused,' he had excused him with characteristic patience. 'You can't really expect him to understand.'

They were so very different, Richard and Adam—although when they were younger they had been the best of friends, almost inseparable. They had gone to the same school, competing good-naturedly for top honours in both academic work and on the sports field. But Adam had always been the dynamic one, the more adventurous, at times even a little wild. Richard had been more serious, applying himself with concentration instead of relying on flashes of brilliance.

They had drifted apart after they had gone up to university. Olivia had never really known what had come between them—though Richard had accidentally let slip, a few years ago, that there had been some sort of incident with Georgina, a few months after her marriage. He hadn't elaborated, and she hadn't liked to ask him any more about it.

Again that mysterious force drew her eyes across the room. Adam was showing no signs of making an early departure—he was talking to a clutch of senior directors from Marston's, one of LTS's major customers. She would have liked to have been able to eavesdrop on *that* conversation.

What *was* he doing here? It seemed unlikely that he would have come all this way just to attend Lex's funeral. Were Richard and Eleanor right in thinking that he was here to cause some kind of trouble? A small shiver scudded down her spine, a premonition of danger...

Anyone watching her would have had little clue to the thoughts that were passing through her head. In that, as in many other ways, she was very much Lex's daughter, a chip off the old block. Tall and slender, she had inherited his slightly patrician features, which made her striking rather than conventionally beautiful.

She wore her honey-gold hair in a neat bob, and used the minimum of make-up to highlight the cool grey of her eyes and soft line of her mouth. She was always elegantly dressed—today her softly tailored black suit and pale grey silk shirt, gently ruffled at the neck, struck just the right note.

A few of the guests had begun to make their polite departure, and at last she managed to snatch a few moments to get away. What she needed was a breath of fresh air—and to be alone. As discreetly as she could she slipped out of the drawing-room, and made her escape down through the quiet gardens.

It was high summer, and Beckside was at its best at this time of year; the roses were in full bloom, their sweet perfume mingling on the soft summer breeze with heliotrope and lavender. Absently she wandered down the gravel paths towards the stream that had given the house its name. There was a white-painted summer-house, shaped like a pagoda, at the water's edge, and she pushed open the door and went inside.

This place was so evocative of her childhood— even the very smell of it; of wood that had been soaked and dried out over countless seasons, of cricket bats and swimming costumes forgotten and left here all through the winter, of canvas-covered chairs heated almost to scorching point by the sun blazing through the windows.

She sat down on one of the chairs, and closed her eyes, letting her mind drift back through the years, remembering .

She had known Adam all her life. When she was a little girl, the three families had been very close. Of course, she had been much younger than the others, but Adam had always been kind to her— and in return she had hero-worshipped him.

She had been just seven years old when his parents had been killed, and in spite of the difference in their ages she had felt as if there was some kind of special bond between them; maybe because she too had lost her mother, although she didn't remember her. And besides she had loved Auntie Lizzie and Uncle George.

He had been away at university then, but Lex had insisted that during the long vacations he should regard their home as his. Eleanor hadn't been too keen on him— she had never said as much, of course, knowing how Lex doted on him, but Olivia had known, in the way a child picked up things that adults thought they were keeping to themselves.

She must have been about fifteen or sixteen when she had first begun to realise that her feelings about him were changing. Until then she had been more interested in horses than the opposite sex, but in the hot-house atmosphere of an all-girls boarding-school adolescence had brought an almost obsessive interest in the mysteries of that fascinating species, the male.

It was hardly surprising, perhaps, that all those soft-focus schoolgirl dreams should have come to be centred around the friend of her childhood days. Intriguingly mature, tantalisingly sophisticated, Adam had seemed the very image of all her romantic fantasies.

At least she had had the sense to realise that he was unlikely to welcome the adoration of a gawky teenager, still suffering the excruciating agony of a spotty chin. And besides, he had had a girlfriend. Some girl with red hair, and a fanciful name... Vania, that was it. Olivia had looked it up in one of those name books, and found out that it was just a fancy version of Jane—that had given her some sort of grim satisfaction at the time, though she couldn't imagine why it should have.

He'd brought Vania down to stay for Christmas— Olivia would have been about seventeen by then. Everyone had thought they would probably get engaged. Olivia had hated her—oh, she was stunning to look at, but she was terribly vain. And she hadn't been at all amused when the old Labrador they had then had stolen her fur slipper—by the time they had rescued it from his basket beside the Aga in the kitchen it had been thoroughly chewed. Adam had been very apologetic, but behind her back he had laughed as much as Olivia. And Vania had faded out of their lives.

By the summer holidays Olivia's spots had gone, and her skinny shape had started to blossom into softer curves. She had let her hair grow, too, so that it curled around her shoulders—she had been really rather proud of it. Coming home that summer, she had been acutely conscious that she was growing up.

She hadn't seen Adam for six months—he had been away on business when she had come home at Easter. He had come over for Sunday lunch, as usual, strolling in with a casual greeting—but she hadn't missed the flicker of surprise in his eyes as he saw her.

She had tried hard to keep her cool, afraid that he would laugh at her. But she had found it hard to be in his presence without blushing, and had sought every opportunity to avoid him. It had probably been inevitable that sooner or later he would guess.

It had been a few weeks later; a Friday afternoon, late July, and the weather was hot. She had come down here to the summer-house to slip into her bikini and go for a swim in the beck. Coming out of the tiny cubby-hole they used as a changing-room, she had almost collided with a hard, masculine body...

'Hello, Angel.'

'Oh!' She felt her cheeks flame a vivid scarlet, far too conscious of the near-nakedness of her body in the skimpy bikini. 'Have you...come to see Dad?' she managed to stammer. 'He's in his study...'

He smiled down at her, an odd light flickering in his dark eyes. 'I know—I've just left him there,' he told her. 'I thought I'd stroll down here and take a swim, as it's such a nice day. You don't mind if I join you?'

'No...of course not.' Her heart was pounding so hard that she was sure he could hear it. There was something...she couldn't quite identify it...something in the way he was looking at her... As if he knew exactly how he was affecting her. But he wasn't laughing.

She stepped away from him, feeling the heat of his gaze as it drifted down over her tender young curves. 'It seems like a long time since I've seen you,' he remarked, a strangely husky note in his voice.

'Yes. Well...you were in America at Easter,' she reminded him, her lashes fluttering down to veil her eyes.

'So I was.' The very air between them seemed to be alive with tension—could he feel it too? 'So...you're home for the holidays, then?'

'Yes.' If only she could manage a slightly more intelligent level of conversation!

'You're not leaving school this year?'

'No—I'm staying on to do my A levels. I'm applying to Keele to do a Business Studies degree.'

He laughed teasingly. 'Ah—you're a swot, then?'

'Oh, not really.' She managed a swift smile, lifting her eyes briefly to his face. 'Lex says that if

I'm going to be a director of the company one day I've got to be able to pull my weight.'

'I see.'

She risked another wary glance up at him from beneath her lashes. The way he was looking at her made her mouth go dry. 'I... I think I'll go and have my swim now,' she stammered, suddenly desperate to escape before those dark eyes could put a spell on her. 'It's... so hot.'

He put out his hand, and caught her arm. 'Why are you in such a hurry to get away from me?' he taunted. 'You really seem to have been trying to avoid me these past couple of weeks.'

'Oh, no—of course not.' *Please* let me go, she was begging inside. Her bones seemed to have turned to jelly, and in a moment she was going to betray herself.

'I could almost have begun to wonder if I'd done something to upset you?'

'Oh, no.'

He laughed softly, knowingly. 'Run along, then,' he said, releasing her arm. 'I'll be out in a minute.'

She darted away from him like a nervous fawn, skittering down to the wooden jetty they used as a swim-platform. The stream was about twenty-five feet wide at this point, and in the middle it was just deep enough for her to be out of her depth. The water was sparklingly clear, babbling down from the limestone peaks, and the willow trees overhanging its banks painted it with dappled shade.

She dived in smoothly, grateful for the coolness of the water to soothe the fever that was racing in her blood. Her body was still on fire from the way he had looked at her. She had been dreaming for so long that he would one day look at her like that, but now...she was frightened. Something older than time had slipped itself between them, like the serpent in the Garden of Eden, and the innocence in their relationship was gone for ever.

She turned over on to her back, paddling gently, watching as he came out of the summer-house. He was wearing the briefest pair of black swimming-trunks, and the sight of his powerful, hard-muscled body almost took her breath away. His skin was bronzed by the sun, and across his broad chest there was a dusting of rough dark hairs. He was all male...

He dived in, making hardly a splash, and sliced beneath the water, coming up a few feet away from her. She laughed a little nervously, and kicked her feet, deliberately splashing him. He responded to the challenge with a grin, snatching at her ankle and pulling her under.

Slickly she twisted out of his grasp, and struck out upstream with a powerful stroke, but he soon caught up with her and gave her another ducking. She came up spluttering and laughing, to find that he was very close... She couldn't quite reach the bottom here, though he could stand, and that gave him an unfair advantage that he did not hesitate to exploit.

They had swum together like this so often before, fooling around and indulging in horse-play, but this time it was very different—they both knew it. It was in the way he held her, letting her test her strength against his but always letting her know that he was the stronger. Every time she had almost caught her breath he would push her under again, until she was weak and half-drowned, having to cling to him helplessly, the heat of his hard male body stirring all sorts of strange sensations inside her. He lifted her out of the water, curving her against him, and as he looked down at her his eyes were suddenly so dark that she felt a shimmer of alarm run through her.

His hands slid around her, holding her close and she could feel the warmth of his breath, fanning her cheek. 'What's happened to you, Angel?' he murmured smokily. 'One minute you were just a kid, all legs like Zadie's colt, and the next   ' With a low groan he dragged her into his arms. 'Oh, Angel, I shouldn't take advantage of you like this. Lex would have me horse-whipped if he knew.'

Her heart seemed to have stopped beating. He was really going to kiss her...

His head lowered, and his mouth claimed hers, warm and firm, just as she had known it would be. The tip of his tongue expertly sought the sensitive corners of her lips, coaxing them gently apart. She closed her eyes, feeling herself melting as everything female in her responded to the unmistakable hunger she could sense in him.

He was curving her supple young body to the hard length of his, and his hand had curled into her wet hair, holding her still as his sensuous tongue swept deep into the secret corners of her mouth. All the tumultuous longings that she had barely understood were flaring to life as the kiss deepened and became more demanding; her head was dizzy with the racing of her blood, and she had to cling to him to stop herself from falling into outer space...

CHAPTER TWO

'HELLO, Angel.'

Olivia sat up quickly, catching her breath at the sound of that sardonic voice.

'Funny, I thought I'd find you here.' Adam moved closer to her, perching on the edge of a wooden table beside her chair.

'What...what are you doing here?' she demanded, her heart thudding with shock.

'Like you, escaping for a moment from prying eyes,' he responded laconically.

'If you didn't want to cause gossip, why did you come back?' she countered, her eyes flickering with cold fire.

'I came back for Lex's funeral. Causing gossip was an unfortunate, but probably inevitable side-effect.'

She laughed drily. 'You're trying to pretend that you care about Lex's death?' she challenged, unable to keep the bitter edge of sarcasm from her voice.

'No, I'm not trying to pretend.' Suddenly those eyes were as hard as black diamonds. 'I *do* care—strange as it may seem to you.'

'Then it's a pity you didn't think about him a little more six years ago,' she threw back at him. 'He thought the sun shone out of you. It almost killed him, what you did. In a way it *did* kill him, the old Lex. He was never the same.'

'If he thought so much of me, why was he so certain, even before the trial, that I was guilty?' he enquired, his voice deceptively soft. 'You were all so convinced, weren't you? Even you. I thought at least *you* might have reserved judgement until you had heard my side of it, but you wouldn't even listen to me. You slammed the phone down on me, remember?'

Oh, yes, she remembered—she remembered every moment, as vividly as if it had been only yesterday. But she wasn't going to let him know that, and she came back fighting. 'Your side of it?' she challenged, a sting of sarcasm in her voice. 'I would have said the evidence was pretty conclusive. It didn't take the jury very long to find you guilty, anyway. A unanimous verdict.'

'And you were there, weren't you?' he countered, his hard mouth curled into a cold smile. 'Oh, yes, I saw you, sitting there in the back row with Richard. Why did you come? They don't feed people to the lions any more, you know—it must have been quite a disappointment for you.'

She forced herself to lean back in her chair, assuming an air of cool indifference. 'It was Richard who wanted to come,' she informed him, a measure of disdain in her voice. 'He wanted to hear it all for himself. Right up to the end, he found it very hard to believe that you could really have done it.'

'Did he really?' What was the meaning of that enigmatic glint in his eyes? 'And now little Ricky has done very well for himself, hasn't he? Chairman of the company, and about to marry a third of the shares... When is the happy day, by the way?' he added mockingly. 'I saw the announcement of your engagement in the papers—it seems to be an awfully long time ago.'

She tilted up her chin, returning the mocking look with cold dignity. 'We haven't set the date yet,' she informed him. 'When we do, I can assure you that you'll be one of the first to know.'

'"When"?' He lifted one dark eyebrow in sardonic enquiry. 'Are you sure it isn't "if"?'

'No, of course not...'

'You don't want to marry him, Angel,' he murmured, his smile taunting her. 'You'd be wasted on him. I bet when he's making love to you he's going through the latest trade figures in his mind.'

'I...' Why couldn't she answer him? What sinister spell was he weaving with the mesmerising power of those dark eyes?

'Yes, wasted.' He put out his hand to stroke down over her cheek, drawing her towards him with a hidden force that was stronger than gravity itself. 'Can you really tell me that you're satisfied with his kisses? Are you sure you haven't been yearning for something more all these years...?'

She stared up at him helplessly. He still held so much power over her, even after all this time. As his head bent towards hers, her lips parted in instinctive response...

'What the hell's going on?' Richard's harsh voice sliced painfully through the magic cloak Adam had spun around her.

Adam laughed, and let her go. 'I'm seducing your fiancée,' he drawled lazily. 'What are you going to do about it?'

Richard looked questioningly from Adam to Olivia, a hurt question in his eyes, and with an enormous effort of will she pulled herself together. 'It was nothing like that,' she asserted in clear, cold tones. She moved over to Richard's side, and linked her hands through his arm, drawing strength from him to regard Adam with aloof contempt. 'There's no point in your being here,' she added levelly. 'You might as well go back to Australia, and leave us alone.'

That cynical smile twisted his hard mouth. 'Such touching loyalty,' he scorned with biting sarcasm. 'You're a lucky man, Ricky. If I were you I'd get the knot tied quickly, before someone comes along and steals her right out from under your nose— with her thirty-three percent of LTS.' He sauntered over to the door, all arrogant self-assurance. 'But I'm sorry to disappoint you—I'm not planning to leave England just yet. In fact I might stick around for quite a while.'

He was gone, the door swinging shut behind him, but that air of menace seemed to linger. Olivia shuddered, and Richard slid his arm around her shoulder, drawing her gently against him.

'Don't let him upset you,' he coaxed. 'It's all just empty threats. He can't hurt us—I won't let him.'

She closed her eyes, letting her forehead rest against his wide shoulder. Dear, reliable Richard— she was so fond of him... Suddenly Adam's taunting words came back to echo in her brain— 'Are you sure you haven't been yearning for something more all these years...?' She drew back out of his embrace, alarmed by the sharp pang of guilt that had assailed her.

'We... We'd better go back inside,' she managed to say. 'Eleanor will be annoyed if we don't pull our weight.'

He smiled warmly down at her. 'Of course—if you're sure you feel up to it?'

She nodded resolutely. 'I'm not going to let Adam Taylor think he can scare us,' she vowed. 'Come on.'

Arm in arm they strolled back up through the gardens—two tall, elegant people, her hair honey-blonde, his light brown, their discreetly expensive clothes worn with style. Everyone always said they were very well matched.

Olivia had always enjoyed riding over the hills early in the morning. It was her favourite time of day, when white shreds of mist still hung in the hollows and the dew made silver jewels of spiders' webs in the grass. Kelly, her young bay mare, moved with a smooth, easy canter over the rising ground. The sky was a clear pale blue, promising another lovely day, and she breathed the sweet morning air with pleasure.

She hadn't slept very well—after the upsets of yesterday she hadn't expected to. Long into the night she had lain awake, her mind filled with troubled thoughts. Why had she almost let Adam kiss her? She had tried to reassure herself that it was only because she had been reliving those old memories—but it had been unsettling, all the same.

Richard hadn't questioned her at all about that scene he had witnessed in the summer-house—he had accepted her assurance that it hadn't been what Adam had claimed. He trusted her implicitly—and that made her feel all the more guilty...

Suddenly the young mare tossed her head, whinnying, and Olivia became aware of the sound of hoof-beats on the ground behind her, gaining on her. She glanced back over her shoulder, catching a fleeting glimpse of a powerful black hunter, with a tall man in the saddle—a man with tousled dark hair, and broad shoulders...

She urged her horse into a gallop; sensing her agitation, the bay flew over the grass, her mane whipping in the wind. But the black horse was gaining inexorably; Adam was leaning up over its withers, perfectly attuned to the animal's motion, controlling it with the lightest touch of his hands on the reins.

The pursuit was swift and fierce. Overhauling her, the black wheeled in front of her, forcing her to swerve and stop. The young bay reared up, frightened, and Adam reached out and caught her bridle, steadying her. Olivia's cool grey eyes flashed him a frost-warning.

'Thank you—I can manage her perfectly well without your help,' she snapped, wishing she was not so out of breath from the chase.

His devil's smile taunted her. 'Good,' he mocked, but he kept his hold on the bridle, making plain his intention that she would not go until he was ready to set her free.

'I thought you'd have gone back to town with Georgina,' she tossed at him, injecting a note of cool indifference into her voice.

He laughed softly. 'Ah, yes—Georgina,' he mused, as if he had almost forgotten the woman's very existence. 'Oh, no—heaven forbid! She has her uses, but a whole afternoon in her company was quite enough, thank you.'

She glared at him. 'What a cold-blooded bastard you are!' But didn't she know that already? Why should she be shocked by the depth of his callousness?

He shrugged his wide shoulders in a gesture of unconcern. 'That's more or less what she said,' he drawled with undisguised arrogance. 'But she'll be there if I need her again.'

'You seem very confident of that,' she retorted tartly, galled to know that he was probably right. She would have liked to have been able to wheel her horse away, but he still gripped her bridle. Kelly had calmed now, and like a traitor was flirting quietly with Adam's big hunter.

He urged the black into a walk, leading the young mare alongside him. Olivia did her best to ignore him, holding her head high in the air, her brittle anger wrapped around her like a shell. How could she ever have thought she was in love with a man like this? He was pure evil.

But the silence that stretched between them was like a void, making her feel uncomfortable. She was too aware of him, close beside her, his thigh almost brushing against hers as the two horses walked along side by side. Numbly her mind sought for

something casual to say, to try to disguise the agitation she was feeling.

There was something familiar about the black
hunter. 'Isn't that General?' she enquired a little
stiffly. 'I thought you'd sold him when...' She
caught herself up, blushing, as she stopped herself
from finishing her sentence.

But Adam had no such inhibitions. 'When I went
to prison, you mean?' he enquired, a glint of dark
humour in his eyes. 'I did—to John Potts.'

'Lex's old groom?'

He nodded. 'He's looked after him well—he must
be all of fifteen years old now, but he's as fit as a
young colt.' He stroked the horse's sleek neck with
one hand. 'I didn't really expect him to remember
me, but as soon as he saw me he went crazy in his
stall. Didn't you, old son?'

The horse turned his head in response to his
voice, and Olivia felt an odd little lump in her
throat. How could a man who could have a rapport
like that with an animal be all bad? But he was,
she reminded herself swiftly. To let herself forget
that, even for a moment, could be very
dangerous...

'I might even buy him back,' Adam mused, half
to himself.

She looked at him in surprise. 'And ship him all
the way to Australia?'

He slanted her an enigmatic smile. 'Ah—but I'm
not at all sure that I'm going to go back to
Australia,' he responded provocatively. 'I'd almost
forgotten about the... attractions of Derbyshire.
Maybe, now that I'm home, I'll stay for good.'

She stared at him, her heart pounding too fast. The look in his eyes suggested that it wasn't just the beauties of the countryside he was referring to. She had been afraid of the prospect that he might stay for a couple of weeks. If he were to stay for ever...!

He had dropped his hand from her bridle, but she made no attempt to escape him—she knew it would be useless, until he was ready to let her go. He was regarding her with sardonic interest, and she braced herself for his next mocking remark.

'So how is your loving fiancé this morning?' he enquired.

She had guessed that sooner or later he would bring Richard into the conversation, and she managed to answer in a commendably level voice, 'He's very well.'

'Left him in bed, have you?'

She half choked, her cheeks flaming scarlet. 'No, I haven't, I...'

'You what?'

She fought for some semblance of composure— Adam Taylor was the last person she wanted to know the intimate details of her personal life.

But those dark eyes were far too perceptive. 'Well, well,' he drawled, a hateful note of mockery in his voice. 'Don't tell me you're not even sleeping with him?'

She swallowed hard. 'We...chose to wait until after we're married.'

'Did you really? And he's been content to wait for three years! I never thought he was such a wet fish!'

She favoured him with an icy glare. 'I'm very happy with Richard,' she informed him with dignity. 'He's a very nice man.'

'*Nice?*' He made the word sound like an insult. 'I was right,' he taunted. 'You're wasted on him. I wouldn't have waited three years for you—and you wouldn't have waited three years for me.' His voice had taken on a husky timbre. 'Every time I kissed you, it was like a fever—remember? It would be very tempting to kiss you now, Angel. The trouble is, I'm not at all sure that I could stop at just kisses. And, while I'm not averse to making love on the grass, I've a feeling we could be seen from the road here.'

Her heart was pounding so hard that she could scarcely breathe. 'You seriously think I'd allow you to make love to me?' she demanded hoarsely.

His eyes glinted with dark fire. 'Oh, I wasn't thinking of asking permission,' he murmured. 'Not that I think you'd refuse.'

'Why, you arrogant...' Without even forming the conscious intention of hitting him, she swung her hand at his face.

He caught it swiftly in mid-air, his fingers closing around hers like a vice. 'Am I?' He drew her hand up to his lips, laying one scalding kiss against the tumultuous pulse inside her wrist, sending a shimmer of heat right through her. 'But you know that I'm right, don't you, my lovely, desirable Angel? There's a certain inevitability about it— there always has been.'

She stared up at him, feeling herself drowning in the depths of those dark, hypnotic eyes. The subtle male muskiness of his skin filled her senses, stirring memories that drugged her mind...

'No, I don't think you'd refuse.'

He let her go, breaking the spell. A hot fury flooded through her, and she had difficulty in controlling Kelly's skittish response to her sudden agitation. 'How *dare* you touch me?' she demanded, her voice shaking. 'Haven't you done enough harm already? Can't you be satisfied? Go away—leave us alone. I hate you.'

That cynical smile taunted her. 'Maybe you do. But you still want me—that's something you just can't control, no matter how hard you try. You know, I could have had Georgina last night—she was mine for the taking. But I didn't want her—I wanted you. And it's going to be good, Angel. Worth waiting six years for.'

A flame of scarlet suffused her cheeks, and she wheeled the young bay sharply away from him, spurring her with her heels into a swift gallop. He made no attempt to follow her, but she could sense him watching her with that mocking gaze, chalking up the first victory to himself.

How could she have been fool enough to let him weave his spells around her again? Hadn't she warned herself, over and over again through the night, that he was dangerous? Oh, he was very clever, she conceded bitterly. He must have had a great deal of experience in the games of seduction, to employ them with such deadly skill. He had spoken of making love to her—without her permission—out here on the open hills, in broad daylight... The image those words had conjured rose vividly in her brain, making her mouth feel suddenly dry.

She shook her head, trying to dispel such traitorous thoughts. No—she would never betray Richard like that. But she was all too uncomfortably aware that the powerful tug of physical attraction was still there, however much she might try to deny it. And she had no more idea of how to control it now than she had had all those years ago...

That first kiss had seemed to be all she had ever dreamed of. But as she clung to him, ready to offer him anything he wanted, he abruptly let her go, pushing her firmly away, and his soft laughter held a mocking note that confused and hurt her. 'This is getting a little crazy,' he warned, as breathless as she was, his eyes glittering with a feral light. 'I didn't intend to let things get so out of hand.'

Her eyes filled with tears as she gazed up at him. 'Adam...' she whispered desperately.

But he was moving away from her. 'I'm sorry, Angel. The heat must have got to my brain. Don't worry—it won't happen again.' And he was gone before she could stop him, cleaving through the water with a powerful stroke that took him swiftly out of her reach, leaving her feeling empty and utterly ashamed. She had behaved so wantonly—he would only despise her now.

She hadn't seen him after that for about two weeks—even Eleanor had remarked several times how unusual it was that he hadn't been over even for Sunday lunch. Olivia had kept quiet, embarrassed by the knowledge that he was staying away because of her, because he didn't want a stupid teenager throwing herself at him again.

And then one afternoon she had been sun-bathing in her bikini again, down by the stream. She had been reading her book, but it was so warm, and she was so sleepy. Her eyes had drifted shut, and she had begun to let herself slip away into that land of magical fantasies...

Suddenly a shadow fell over her eyes, and she opened them to find Adam standing above her. Her heart bounced in shock, and she sat up quickly, hugging her knees in some kind of instinctive de-fensiveness, shimmeringly aware once again of every curve of her body, so very inadequately con cealed by the tiny scraps of coloured fabric. If only she had her T-shirt within reach...

He smiled slowly, a strange smile that made her spine shiver. 'Hi, Angel,' he greeted her, stretching himself out on the grass beside her, his head propped up on his hand. 'Lovely afternoon, isn't it?'

'Yes, it... it is,' she managed to stammer.

'Enjoying your holiday?'

'Yes, thank you.'

He laughed, low in his throat, and reached up to coil one finger into a long strand of her blonde hair. 'You seem very tense,' he murmured, the huskiness of his voice reaching chords of response deep inside her. 'What's wrong?'

She felt her cheeks flame a heated scarlet, and lowered her eyes. 'Nothing... I...'

He was watching her with those dark, mesmer-ising eyes, and she felt as if she was being hypnotised. 'Yes, there is—and we both know what it is.' His fingers had tangled into her hair, and she couldn't have got away even if she had wanted to. 'I've tried to stay away from you, Angel,' he growled. 'I was afraid I'd be tempted into something I know I should resist. You're far too young yet...'

Her mouth was dry, and she could scarcely breathe. What was it he knew he should resist...? He was tugging gently at her hair, drawing her inexorably down to him, and again she was vividly conscious of his hard male strength, of the evocative musky scent of his body that was filling her senses, drugging her mind.

'You're such a little innocent...' He stroked his hand lightly over her cheek. 'But so ready for love...' His thumb brushed over her trembling lips, parting them, and he drew her down into his arms, his mouth claiming hers in a deep, sensuous kiss, to which she could only surrender.

He had laid her back in the long grass; his body was hard and heavy, half crushing her beneath his weight, and his tongue was plundering deep into her mouth, invading every sweet secret in a kiss that was far too adult for her innocence to resist.

'Oh, Angel...' His breathing was harsh and ragged as he burrowed into the hollow of her shoulder, unerringly finding the sensitive hollows where her racing pulse fluttered beneath her skin. 'You've grown up so beautiful...'

His hand was smoothing down over her slender curves with a lazy possessiveness, as if every inch had long been promised to him. All the incoherent longings that had been troubling her for months awoke, and her body curved towards him in unknowing invitation. His mouth was ravaging hers with a fierce demand against which there could be no defence, plumbing all the deepest corners, demanding all she had to give, and with slow, sensuous strokes he was tracing circles over the peach-smooth plain of her stomach, higher and higher, with an unmistakable intent.

She whimpered softly, half in anticipation and half in fear, as those long, clever fingers rose to mould her small, ripe breast, barely covered by the taut jersey fabric of her bikini. Something strange was happening, a sweet, swelling ache of response, and the tender bud of her nipple had hardened beneath his palm. He brushed it with his thumb, laughing low in his throat, a sound of mingled triumph and satisfaction, as if he knew that no other man had ever touched her like this before.

His eyes were dark with a warning message as they gazed down into hers—but she wasn't yet fluent in the language they were speaking. She knew only the sweet tide of feminine submissiveness that was flooding through her, and he smiled slowly as he recognised it. His gaze wandered hungrily over her slender curves, and then returned to rest at the small bow at the front of the bikini top, nestling between her breasts.

She didn't know that she was holding her breath as he took one end of the tie between his fingers, and drew it slowly undone, as if he were unwrapping a gift-wrapped parcel. The hook that kept the skimpy thing fastened was beneath the bow, and with deft fingers he unfastened it. A quiver of tension ran through her as he brushed the fabric aside.

It seemed like an eternity that she lay in his arms as his burning eyes lingered over the ripe swell of her naked young breasts. She had tanned slightly in her bikini, so the skin that had been covered was a little creamier by contrast, more vulnerable, and the pink peaks stood pert and hard, provocatively inviting his touch.

With one fingertip, tantalisingly light, he began to trace a circle over one aching mound. She let her breath go in a long, sobbing sigh, and he smiled down into her eyes. 'You're almost a woman now, Angel,' he murmured, his voice smoky from the fires in his eyes. 'So close... It isn't fair to ask a man to wait...'

His head bent over her breast, and a shock of heat jolted through her as she felt his moist, rough tongue lap at the sensitive nipple. His teeth nibbled gently, darting a million sparks of fire into her brain, and then he took the whole of the succulent berry into his mouth, suckling deeply, swirling her down into a giddying vortex where only these exquisite sensations were real.

She was curving herself against him, her fingers tangled in his tousled dark hair as she offered him her total surrender. He had moved on top of her, his thighs parting hers, the rough fabric of his cotton trousers rasping against her soft skin, and his name was on her lips as she pleaded for something she didn't even understand.

But then he raised his head, and the groan that broke from his lips seemed to hold real pain. 'Oh, my God, Angel, we shouldn't be doing this.'

'Please, Adam. I love you,' she whispered brokenly. 'Please...'

He lifted his weight from her, and with a tender hand he brushed the hair back from her face. 'Do you?' he asked, smiling in a way she didn't quite understand.

'Yes.' Was he going to say that she was too young to be in love? But she knew that she wasn't—she knew that this was real, this was forever.

That smile was so strange... 'Well, I didn't intend that it should be quite so soon,' he murmured softly. 'But we certainly can't go on like this. I think you're going to have to marry me.'

She stared up at him in total bewilderment. Had he really said that, or was she dreaming...?

He laughed wryly. 'I've taken you rather by surprise, haven't I?' he murmured on a note of gentle teasing. 'I meant to wait until you were a little older—seventeen is really rather too young. And Lex is likely to go off the deep end at the mere idea.'

'You...you really *mean* it?' she whispered, still hardly daring to believe it.

'Of course I mean it.' He dropped a light kiss on the tip of her nose. 'So—is the answer yes?'

'Oh, yes.' She could barely speak for the breathless fluttering of her heart. 'Oh, *yes.*'

His sensual mouth melted over hers again, stirring again with consummate ease the fires of hunger inside her. But he had himself well under control now, and though he was reducing her to a state of molten helplessness he made sure that he didn't let things go too far.

'No—we're going to do this properly,' he insisted, gently easing her away from him and rising to his feet, pulling her up with him. 'Lex would string me up if he thought I was jumping the gun.'

'Do you ... do you think he might not want us to get married?' she asked, lifting wide, anxious eyes to his face.

He smiled wryly. 'In another year or two he'd probably be delighted,' he surmised. 'But right now ... After all, you're only seventeen—and I'm twenty-eight. It's quite a big age-gap.'

'Yes. I ... I suppose it is.' Her lashes fluttered down to shadow her flushed cheeks. He was going to change his mind—how fleeting the dream had been! But he lifted her into his arms again, burying his face in her hair.

'I really ought to give you time to be sure, Angel,' he husked, and there was no mistaking the urgency in his voice and in his body. 'You're awfully young to be taking such a big step as marriage. But I want you so much—if I don't marry you, I'm likely to do something far worse.'

A surge of pure joy rose inside her. He meant it—incredible as it seemed, Adam loved her, and he wanted to marry her. 'I don't need time,' she whispered, reaching up to wrap her arms tightly around his neck. 'I love you—I've been in love with you for ages. And Lex will agree—I know he will. And if he doesn't, we could ... we could run away together.'

He laughed softly, shaking his head. 'No, we'll persuade him. He'll probably end up thinking it was his idea in the first place!'

He bent his head again to claim her mouth in a long, lingering, tender kiss, and she responded with all her heart. But though she curved herself against him, her slender young body supplicant against the hard length of his, she knew that his self-discipline was stronger than his animal need. It thrilled her to try to provoke him, moving against him in seductive invitation, sensing the dangerous power of a fierce male demand barely held in check.

He grasped her wrists, breaking her hold around his neck, and pushed her firmly away. 'You'd better go,' he rasped, the dark fire in his eyes warning her not to risk any more. 'If you stay here much longer, you won't be able to wear white in church.' With a wry smile he drew the two halves of her bikini-top back together, and fastened it. 'And don't wear this again when I'm around,' he added huskily, 'or I won't be responsible for the consequences. There's a limit to how much temptation flesh and blood can stand.' He turned her around, and sent her on her way with a gentle pat on her dainty behind. 'Go on, run along indoors. It's nearly lunchtime anyway.'

She pouted, not wanting to be sent away like a child. But the glint in his eyes told her that he certainly didn't see her as a child. For a moment she hesitated, torn between her own hunger, urging her to stay, and the primeval fear of a young and vulnerable female faced with a very aroused male. The fear won, and she snatched up her T-shirt and ran, back up through the rough grass to the cultivated part of the garden and in through the back door of the house.

Had it all been a dream? It was so sudden, so unexpected. How could he be in love with her? He was a grown man, he had been around, he had had dozens of beautiful women in his life... Could he really want to marry a kid of seventeen...?

What a naïve little fool she had been, she cursed herself bitterly. It shouldn't have taken much intelligence to realise why he had been so keen to marry her: she was Lex's sole heir, standing to inherit one third of LTS—and that would have given him absolute control.

He had been quite ruthless in the way he had used her inexperience to lure her into his snare, playing with her emotions and deliberately arousing her body to adult desires that she had been too young to handle. Of course, the fact that she was a virgin had probably given the game an extra attraction for him—she had learned that that kind of thing appealed to some men.

A shiver of heat ran through her. He was still playing the same games—and, though she might wish to deny it, she was as vulnerable as ever.

CHAPTER THREE

OLIVIA stood at the window of her office, gazing down over the roofs of the buildings that made up the hub of the Lambert, Taylor & Simpson empire. The executive offices were on the top floor of the front building, and behind lay the workshops. Lex had believed that keeping everything so close preserved the traditions of a family firm—it had been his proud boast that he knew every one of his employees by name.

Of course, times had changed, the firm was growing; Richard had taken over a number of smaller firms in the region since he had been chairman. It wasn't to be expected that he could keep the degree of personal contact with the workforce that Lex had always maintained. But it was a shame that the old atmosphere had gone...

'You're looking a little pale this morning, Olivia.' She turned, startled, at the sound of Richard's voice—she hadn't heard him open the connecting door between their two offices. He came across the room, and dropped a light kiss on her cheek, smiling down at her in concern. 'Are you feeling well?' he asked. 'You needn't have come into the office—I could manage without you for the rest of the week if you'd like to take a few days off.'

'Oh... no.' She shook her head. 'I'm fine. It's just... well, yesterday *was* a bit of a strain, Adam showing up at the funeral like that.' Something jerked sharply at her conscience. Why hadn't she mentioned meeting him while she was out riding? It wasn't like her to keep secrets from Richard...

Richard smiled back at her, suspecting nothing. 'I shouldn't let him worry you,' he remarked dismissively. 'I think he'll find that I'm more than a match for any tricks of his.'

'You really think that he might be intending to cause trouble?' she asked, pretending a deep interest in attending to the task of plucking out the withered leaves from a coleus on the windowsill to hide the unwelcome blush of colour that had risen to her cheeks.

'I don't know. He'll be a fool if he does—he can't hurt us without killing the goose that lays his own golden eggs.'

'You don't think that maybe he just wants to...make some contribution to the running of the company?' she suggested tentatively.

'He hasn't taken much of an interest these past six years,' Richard pointed out with a touch of asperity. 'I can't see why he should suddenly want to start interfering now.'

'Except that...well, Lex was around before— even though he didn't take a very active part in running things. But Adam may feel...'

'That things are different now? Oh, I don't doubt that he still thinks I'm incapable of doing anything as well as he could.' The wry humour in his voice showed his total lack of bitterness. 'Besides, can you see Adam being content to work with me as chairman?'

Olivia smiled, shaking her head. She really couldn't imagine that! 'Maybe he's just bored,' she mused—it wasn't easy to keep just the right note of indifference in her voice. 'All that sunshine—it must get tedious, day after day with nothing to do but sit around on the beach.'

Richard's smile reflected wry amusement. 'He should be so lucky! When was the last time either of us had a proper break? Apart from the weekend of my cousin's wedding, we've neither of us had a weekend off since Christmas!'

Olivia smiled up at him fondly. '*I* have—I've had several,' she reminded him. 'But you—you're in danger of becoming a workaholic. You didn't even come with me to visit Corinna and David.'

His blue eyes danced with humour. 'Ah—well, to be honest, I was glad of an excuse to get out of that,' he confessed. 'Weekends with your old school-friends are not exactly my idea of heaven.'

She flashed him a look of mock-anger, but she understood his point of view. When she and Corinna got together they *were* inclined to chatter on for hours, blissfully unaware that anyone else would be bored stiff with their endless recollections of the minor pranks of their peers and the eccentricities of their teachers.

Richard slipped his arms around her waist from behind, drawing her back against him. 'I've been thinking—maybe it's time we did take a break,' he suggested, smiling down at her. 'Why don't we take a few days off? Perhaps we could go over to Paris.'

She blinked up at him in surprise. 'Could we?' she asked. 'I mean, I know how busy you are...'

He laughed softly. 'Oh, I think I could manage to get away for a few days,' he said. 'For our honeymoon.'

'Our *honeymoon*?' The suggestion was so un-expected that she was completely taken aback. 'But... I mean... Don't you think it's a bit soon after the funeral?' she protested, moving away from him.

'A little, maybe,' he conceded. 'But I think people would understand. We have waited an awfully long time, Olivia. And besides,' he added with a wry smile, 'are you sure that you really want to go on sharing the house with Eleanor, now that Lex is gone?'

That was certainly a point. Although the house would ultimately be hers, it had been left to Eleanor for her lifetime, and already she was making elab-orate plans for redecoration. Olivia hadn't said anything, but it didn't seem to her to be quite right to be rushing so quickly to change everything.

'Well, I——'

'I don't mean right this minute,' Richard urged, taking both her hands in his. 'There's the banns to be read, and people to be invited—and I dare say it'll take a week or two for you to get your dress made. Why don't we say the middle of September?'

'The middle of September?'

'That's six weeks away. Does that give you enough time?'

'Enough time?' She seemed unable to do any-thing but repeat what he was saying—her mind was a whirlpool of confusion. Vivid images were rising from memory to taunt her—images of Adam, with

his sardonic smile, talking about making love to
her on the grass...

'Olivia?' Richard's serious blue eyes looked down
into hers, searching them anxiously. 'You haven't
changed your mind, have you?' he asked.

He lifted her left hand, so that a beam of sunlight caught the sparkling diamond on her third
finger, reminding her that she had already
promised. She couldn't let Adam come between
them, not after all this time. It just wouldn't be
fair...

'Of course I haven't changed my mind,' she assured him quickly, smiling up at him in warm
affection. 'It was just... a bit of a surprise, that's
all. It isn't like you to be so impulsive!'

His look of relief rewarded her. He dropped a
light kiss on her forehead. 'Well, maybe I should
be impulsive a little more often,' he suggested,
chuckling. 'So, what do you think? A September
wedding?'

She nodded, refusing to listen to any guilty
whispers in the darkest corners of her mind. 'Yes—
that would be lovely. Of course, it'll be quite a
rush—there'll be an awful lot to do. We'd better let
Eleanor know right away, and start thinking about
the guest-list.'

'I'll leave all that to you,' he said. 'Perhaps you'd
better take the rest of the day off, and start to make
the arrangements.'

'Yes. I'll ring Eleanor, and we can have lunch
together. And you'd better ring Reverend Peter at
St Michael's—we ought to make an appointment
to see him as soon as possible.'

Richard turned to his desk, and flicked over his diary. 'I could make it on Thursday afternoon,' he suggested. 'Are you free then?'

Olivia smiled with wry amusement; she knew Richard didn't mean to sound as if he was only just able to fit in something so very important. He had always worked too hard; after they were married, she would try to make sure he took time to relax a little more.

'Thursday will be fine,' she agreed. 'I'll go and ring Eleanor.'

'If there's nothing else then, miss, I'll be getting away home—Tom has just come for me.'

Olivia glanced up from the document she was reading. 'Oh—yes, of course, Dee. Thank you. I'll make myself some coffee later if I want some.'

'Goodnight then, miss.'

The housekeeper withdrew, and a few moments later Olivia heard the sound of her husband's car pulling away down the long gravel drive. She leaned back in her armchair, and closed her eyes. The house was empty—it was Eleanor's bridge night, and she certainly wasn't one to let a small thing like the loss of a husband interfere with her social life.

It was a week since the funeral—a week since she and Richard had set the date for their wedding. It had been a frantic week—there had been no time for second thoughts. From the moment she had told Eleanor, it had seemed as if everything had moved out of her control—as if she had stepped on to a fast-moving escalator, and was being whipped along at breakneck speed, unable to step off.

Eleanor had thought the idea was an excellent one—it had probably occurred to her too that it would be a way of getting the house to herself, Olivia guessed shrewdly. She had immediately plunged into organising everything, and Olivia had found herself being hustled around to dressmakers and florists, car-hire firms and stationery printers.

Of course Eleanor had been in her element—organising an occasion like this was exactly suited to her talents. And if she was a little inclined to take over, and make all the decisions...well, it was easier to just let her get on with it. It wasn't as if she had any very firm ideas herself about what she wanted.

And so Olivia had found herself obliged to agree that she needed no fewer than five bridesmaids, and a pageboy as well; and the initial guest-list had crept up to nearly three hundred—many of them distant relatives whom she could hardly recall if she had ever met.

It was a little different to the last time, she reflected with a smile of wry humour. Then Eleanor had made no secret of the fact that she disapproved. She was far too young, she had insisted. But then of course she had never liked Adam. He'd always used to call her Miss Ellie, and that had infuriated her.

And the way he had teased her for her snobbishness had really got her back up. There had been one occasion, years ago, when he had been at university; he had brought a friend home, introducing him only as Algy. Eleanor hadn't been at all impressed by the young man's scruffy appearance—she had commented, none too discreetly, that he looked as if he had bought all his clothes in a jumble-sale. She had been livid when Adam had casually told her that Algy's father was a duke. After that her behaviour towards him had been so obsequious that even Lex had laughed.

She sighed wistfully—there had been a lot of laughter when Adam was around... Impatiently she shook that thought from her brain, and forced herself to turn her attention back to the papers she was trying to study. Richard had targeted another local firm for a take-over bid. This was a much bigger step than anything they had undertaken before, and she wanted to have every detail at her fingertips. But as the ornate ebonised mantel-clock heavily ticked away the hours she was finding it hard to concentrate.

Maybe Eleanor was right about having the house redecorated—this room was rather too heavy for her taste. It had been Lex's study; plush green velvet curtains swathed the tall windows that looked out over the garden and the valley, and the desk was of ornate Victorian walnut marquetry... But, of course, she wouldn't be living here much longer. After she was married to Richard, she would be moving over to his house...

Eleanor came in at about half-past eleven, and put her head round the door to say goodnight. 'Are you planning to stay up much later?' she enquired.

'No—I'll be coming up in a minute.'

'Well, do try and be quiet,' Eleanor pleaded thinly, putting a hand to her brow. 'I've got one of my headaches coming on. I had to partner Polly Wyngate tonight—no one else would—and she really is quite impossible! She will keep butting in when she hasn't got a strong enough suit, and of course she's immediately doubled.'

'Why don't you take one of your pills?' murmured Olivia with routine sympathy.

'Yes, I think I might,' Eleanor agreed. 'Well, goodnight, dear. Don't work too hard.'

'I won't.'

But it was almost one o'clock when finally she set the thick file aside. With a yawn she stood up, collecting up all her papers and returning them to the wall-safe, swinging the hinged bookshelf back across it so that it was cleverly hidden from any but the most astute eye,

She was tired—she had worked on the papers longer than was really necessary. But she had been having trouble sleeping these past few nights, and her dreams had been filled with strange and disturbing images. To try and help herself relax a little she ran herself a warm bath, generously laced with her favourite perfumed oil.

Sinking down into the water, she closed her eyes, and tried to think pleasant thoughts. But her mind was still wound up like a watch-spring, ticking over the same repetitive questions, to which there didn't seem to be an answer.

She *was* doing the right thing in marrying Richard...wasn't she? She did love him—oh, maybe not in the intense, physical way she had loved Adam... But that had been just a silly adolescent infatuation—it would have been a disastrous basis for a marriage.

No, what she shared with Richard was something much more valuable and lasting. It had been Richard who had been there through those black days of despair after Adam had been arrested, when Lex had been so ill. He had always been gentle with her, never putting any pressure on her. It had seemed the most natural thing in the world to become engaged to him.

And he had never once overstepped the mark. They had agreed from the beginning that they would wait until after they were married to...begin the physical side of their relationship. Well...they hadn't actually *discussed* it, as such, but it had been understood.

Though sometimes...she couldn't help but wonder why he had never tried any harder to persuade her. It was stupid, of course, but...he *did* find her attractive in that way, didn't he? She didn't want to be placed on a pedestal, not all the time...

Oh, she was just suffering from a case of pre-wedding nerves, she scolded herself, shaking her head. Of course it would be all right once they were married. Stepping out of the bath, she reached for a thick, fluffy towel, and began to rub herself briskly dry.

The gilt-framed mirror on the wall reflected back an image of her body through the steam, and she rubbed a patch clear, standing back to regard herself in critical appraisal. Not since her teens had she particularly concerned herself with her looks, but now, as she twisted and turned before the mirror, studying herself from every angle, she wished she could see herself as others would see her—as a man would see her...

She wasn't bad-looking—no beauty, perhaps; her nose was a little too long, her chin a little too forceful. But her skin was smooth and clear, and her hair was naturally blonde, with a soft silkiness—she ran her hand through it, letting it trickle down slowly through her fingers. And her body...well, a lot of men liked tall women. And she had quite a decent figure; maybe a little broad in the shoulders—she turned slightly sideways to lessen the effect—but her breasts were firm and shapely, and her legs long and slim.

But was she attractive to men? It wasn't very easy to tell. Oh, some of them flattered her, and occasionally tried to flirt with her, but as a wealthy woman, and a woman in business, she could never quite be sure of what their true motives were.

It was because of Adam that she had never quite grown out of that adolescent uncertainty. He had caught her up at a time when her confidence was just beginning to blossom, and his betrayal had completely undermined her, leaving her never knowing whom she could trust. Perhaps that was why she loved Richard, she acknowledged wryly. He felt safe; she had known him all her life, and he had always treated her with respect...

Respect. She stood still and gazed at her reflection levelly. Such a dry little word. Maybe that was the problem—maybe if Richard had shown a little less restraint, maybe if they had already been lovers, she might not be so vulnerable to Adam's cynical seduction.

A tide of heat flooded her veins as she remembered the way he had spoken of making love to her, out on the hills, without her permission... What if he had tried to carry out his threat? Would she have been able to stop him...?

What was that noise? She caught her breath sharply, her heart thudding in alarm, the small hairs on the back of her head standing on end. Surely... it couldn't possibly be a burglar—she had set the security-alarm herself before coming up to bed.

Maybe she had been mistaken; it had been a very quiet noise—a kind of soft scraping sound. It was probably nothing—a branch in the garden perhaps, moving in the wind. But she couldn't quite dismiss it from her mind, and she knew she wouldn't rest until she had checked to make sure.

Tense with a hundred superstitions that she told herself firmly were stupid and irrational, she reached for her silk wrap, and then, arming herself rather foolishly with a tennis-racket as she crept through the bedroom, she tiptoed downstairs to the hall.

There was a chink of light showing beneath the study door. Had she forgotten to turn it off? Maybe she should call the police right away from the phone in the drawing-room... But she was going to feel awfully silly if she had dragged them all the way out here for nothing. And besides, no one could have got in—there were locks on all the windows, and the winking red light in the corner of the hall told her the burglar alarm was working.

Resolutely gripping the tennis-racket, she tiptoed along the hall, and pushed the door of the study quietly open. As she cast her eyes swiftly around the room she paled in shock. The bookshelf that masked the wall-safe stood ajar, and the safe was wide open. And there, sitting comfortably in Lex's big leather armchair, his feet casually propped on a low coffee-table, reading his way through a pile of confidential papers, was Adam.

He was dressed like a burglar, all in black, with soft-soled shoes that would enable him to move silently. As she stood on the threshold, her eyes wide with shock, he looked up at her, and that cynical mouth curved in a sardonic smile.

'Hi, Angel. Isn't this rather a strange time of night to be playing tennis?' he taunted.

'What the...? How did you get in here?' she demanded furiously.

His dark eyes glinted with mocking amusement. 'Oh, it's just one of the little tricks I learned while I was in prison,' he drawled. 'It's quite an academy, you know, especially as there's so little else to do.'

She stared at him, still stunned. 'But... What are you doing?'

'A little detective work.' He held up the sheaf of papers in his hand—the detailed financial reports that she herself had been reading earlier. 'It makes very interesting reading, this. Much more informative than those nice sanitised company reports.'

'But... How dare you?' Suddenly she came to life, and stalked across the room to snatch the papers from his hand. 'These are private papers. You've broken open my safe——'

'I haven't *broken* it open,' he protested, with the hurt air of a maligned craftsman. 'It was really rather a neat job. I don't think much of your alarm system.'

'It's the best there is.'

'It's years out of date. Any thirteen-year-old with a screwdriver and a bit of fuse-wire could bypass it in under twenty seconds.'

She glared at him in cold fury. 'I'm not going to stand here discussing this with you,' she snapped. 'If you don't get out of here at once, I'll call the police.'

He lifted one dark eyebrow in sardonic enquiry. 'And have me arrested for breaking and entering?' he appealed mockingly. 'With my record, they'd probably give me another six months!'

'You should have thought of that before you broke in here,' she retorted tartly—but her hand, which had been reaching out towards the telephone on the desk, fell back. He noted his victory with a dark gleam of satisfaction, and resumed his calm perusal of her papers.

'So—Richard's planning to take over Mike Sauter's firm?' he enquired. His tone of voice clearly betrayed his scorn.

She tilted up her chin. 'Yes. Do you have some objection?'

'Only that according to these papers it's little better than asset-stripping,' he retorted bluntly. 'Of course there's a nice little profit in it for the company—not to mention eliminating some of the competition—but what about people's jobs? You're going to be looking at large-scale redundancies here. Was Lex aware of what you had in mind?'

She hesitated for only a fraction of a second, re-membering Lex's acid words on the subject. 'Yes, of course he was,' she asserted, tilting her chin in defiance.

Adam's perceptive eyes glinted knowingly. 'But he didn't much like it, did he?' he challenged. 'And what about you? Is this the kind of ruthless man-agement style you favour these days? Or do you just go along with whatever Richard wants?'

She glared back at him in angry defiance, re-fusing to admit that she had disagreed with Richard quite fundamentally over the issue. She knew exactly what he was trying to do—he was trying to drive a wedge between her and Richard by high-lighting the few things they disagreed on. Well, she wasn't going to let him succeed. She would back Richard all the way.

'If you've *quite* finished with your insults, I want you out of here,' she enunciated in glacial accents. 'If you don't go, I shall be obliged to call the police.'

She moved towards the telephone again, but with a startlingly swift movement he was on his feet, and his hand caught her wrist before she could pick up the receiver. 'I'm sorry, but I can't allow you to do that,' he said, a soft hint of menace in his voice. 'I've no intention of going back to prison.'

She lifted her eyes to stare up at him, her mouth suddenly dry with alarm. His fingers were around her wrist like a vice, bruising the delicate skin, but it wasn't only a physical threat he posed. As he had moved closer to her, she had scented the subtle male muskiness of his skin, remembered from so long ago, and some chord of instinct deep inside her had responded immediately.

He must have sensed her reaction, because he smiled slowly, and let his dark gaze drift down over her in an insolent survey. And suddenly she was aware that the sheer peach silk of her wrap did little to disguise the soft contours of her body.

She tried to step back, but she was trapped against the desk, and he still held her captive by her wrist. 'You know, it wasn't very wise of you to come in here dressed like that, Angel,' he murmured, his voice low and smoky. 'I told you once, a long time ago, there's only just so much temptation a man can stand...'

She stood transfixed by the hypnotic darkness of his eyes. The way he called her Angel like that... it brought back so many memories...

'And you've grown even more beautiful since then,' he went on, huskily seductive. 'You were still half a child, barely ripe, so erotic in your innocence. But now you're all woman...' He reached out one hand to cup the soft weight of her breast. 'And infinitely more desirable.'

He was challenging her to protest, but she couldn't utter a sound. The pad of his thumb brushed tantalisingly over the tender peak, and a shimmer of response that she couldn't disguise ran through her. With a low growl he dragged her into his arms, one hand wrapping into her hair to force back her head, so that her body was curved hard against his in a vulnerable arc, and his mouth closed ruthlessly over hers.

His kiss was cruel and demanding, bruising her lips and plundering without mercy into the deepest corners of her mouth, an uninvited invasion that she fought with all the strength she had to resist. But he was far too strong for her. He had curved her back against the desk, so that the hard wooden edge was cutting into the back of her thighs. Her wrap had slid from her shoulders, uncovering one creamy breast, tipped with tender pink. His hand caressed the warm swell with rough possess-iveness—and to her shame and horror she felt a leap of excitement, which she knew had communi-cated itself instantly to him.

His mouth broke from hers, and he laughed in mocking triumph. 'I want you, Angel,' he grated, his voice ragged. 'You know I'm not going to let you marry Richard . . .'

'I am,' she protested, her voice choking. 'It's all arranged——'

'No! You belong to me. You always have. And I'm not going to let you go. Come away with me. We'll live in sin together—wicked, glorious sin!'

She was shaking her head, refusing to listen to what he was saying, trying in vain to push him away. But he was laughing as he subdued her struggles, and she felt herself weakening, betrayed by an in-stinct of pure feminine submissiveness that was as old as Eve.

'Do you know, when I was in prison I used to lie on my bunk and imagine you were there, so real I could feel your body naked beneath me, feel your warm breasts swelling into the palm of my hand, feel your thighs yielding to mine . . .'

He was matching the action to the words, tugging open her wrap as he pushed her down across the desk, his powerful thighs between hers, forcing them apart.

'I hated you for having no faith in me,' he grated, his caresses almost cruel. 'But I still wanted you. I'd been so restrained, holding back from taking you because you were such an innocent little thing, and I didn't want to frighten you. And then you got engaged to Richard—*Richard*!' His eyes glittered with a feral light. 'And of course I assumed that he was enjoying all the sweet, ripening fruits that I'd denied myself. But now I find that it isn't so.' Suddenly he gathered her up in his arms, all fierce tenderness. 'You can't imagine what knowing something like that does to a man, Angel,' he rasped. 'I've waited a long, long time...'

Dear God, he was going to take her here and now, across the desk—and she didn't even want to try to stop him! Her head tipped back dizzily, everything in her aching to surrender to his demand...

A loud crash from the hall broke them abruptly apart. 'Damn!' came Eleanor's voice, thick with drugged sleep. 'Stupid vase—who put it there?'

Dragging her wrap, and the scattered threads of her composure, swiftly around her, Olivia ran to the door. Eleanor was on her knees, clumsily trying to pick up the shattered pieces of a green Chinese vase that had stood for many years on a small table in the hall. 'Oh... It's you,' she gasped foolishly. 'What's happened?'

Eleanor peered up at her, bleary-eyed. 'I thought I heard a noise. Those stupid pills don't work—I still can't sleep, even if I take two. What are you doing still up? Surely you've not been working till this hour?'

'No, I...I thought I might have forgotten to close the safe properly, so I just slipped down to check on it. That must have been what you heard. Here, let me do that—you go back to bed, Eleanor.'

'Yes, I think I will—though I'm sure I won't sleep a wink.' She rose unsteadily to her feet. 'Goodnight, dear—don't forget to turn the lights off.'

'Goodnight, Eleanor.' Olivia watched her stepmother weave her way slowly up the stairs, reflecting that she would be lucky if the pills she had swallowed didn't take effect before she got back to her bed.

'"I thought I might have forgotten to close the safe properly"?' taunted a soft voice from behind her. 'Not, "Adam's raping me across the desk in the study"?'

She turned to face him, the angry defiance in her eyes refusing to acknowledge that by lying to Eleanor she had given herself away. 'You'd better go now,' she insisted, injecting several degrees of frost into her voice. 'Next time I'll call the police first, and ask questions afterwards.'

He shook his head, smiling with arrogant amusement. 'No, you won't, Angel,' he asserted. 'If I'd harboured any doubts at all, you've answered them all. You're not going to marry Richard.'

'Yes, I am. The date's set, all the invitations have gone out——'

'That doesn't mean a thing,' he dismissed, unruffled. 'But we won't discuss it any more tonight—I think I've made my point for now.'

With a mocking smile he stepped past her, making no further attempt to touch her, and went over to the cupboard that concealed the burglar-alarm box. With swift dexterity he removed whatever it was he had used to beat the system, and then with a last meaningful wink he opened the front door, and was gone.

CHAPTER FOUR

It was the middle of the morning. The rush-hour was long past, and the roads into Derby were quiet. The countryside looked so pretty in full leaf, a different shade of green for every tree and field. The powerful V12 engine of the dark blue Jaguar ate up the miles with ease; Richard hadn't been sure that she would be able to handle such a big car, but Olivia found it very comfortable to drive.

For a fleeting moment, the thought came into her mind that she could just go on driving—driving for ever, leaving behind all the guilt, all the doubts and uncertainties that had been torturing her all weekend, leaving behind the past and the future...

It was three days since Adam had broken into the house, and she hadn't been able to bring herself to tell Richard what had happened. How could she ever find the words to explain it? Even if she had censored it a bit, she would still have had to find some reason why she hadn't called the police at once, why she had lied to Eleanor. How would he be able to trust her, after that?

But she was going to have to tell him. With the Sauter deal coming up, she ought to warn him that Adam had seen the papers, knew all about it. And besides, Adam was perfectly capable of telling him himself, and that would be even worse, driving a further wedge of mistrust between them.

Well, she wouldn't give him that chance, she vowed resolutely. She would tell Richard this morning. She should never have delayed so long. He would understand—of course he would. He knew she would never willingly betray him.

She parked her car in her reserved space, next to Richard's beige BMW. It was unusual for her to be so late, but no one commented on it as she walked into the building. The receptionist greeted her with a polite good morning as she crossed the foyer and stepped into the executive lift to ride up to the top floor.

Her secretary looked up from her desk with a smile as she opened the door. 'Oh, hello, Olivia— I wasn't sure if you were coming in today,' she said. 'Would you like me to fetch you a coffee?'

'Oh...yes, please, Elaine. And...by the way, do you happen to know if Mr Simpson is free?'

'I think he's in a meeting—shall I ring his secretary and see if he can be interrupted?'

'No... No, it's all right, Elaine, it isn't that important. Just...leave a message for him to pop in and see me when he's free, would you?'

She went into her own office, and closed the door. There was a pile of letters awaiting her attention, and her diary warned her that she had a meeting after lunch to discuss the company's advertising policy for the next year—she really must study the reports on that before the meeting.

Elaine brought in her coffee, and she sat down, trying hard to make her mind focus on the matters in hand. Usually she enjoyed her work very much. Since she had graduated from her business studies course two years ago she had taken her place in the company as Lex's representative, in anticipation of the day when she would inherit his share of it.

She concentrated mainly on the marketing side; sometimes the men she had to deal with were a little patronising when they first met her, but she could soon show them that she knew as much about the engineering business as they did, and she knew that she was earning respect, not just as Lex's daughter, but in her own right.

But today her mind kept wandering... Elaine had placed a bowl of fresh freesias on her desk, right in a patch of sunlight, and their delicate perfume filled the air. She had made a lot of small changes to this office since she had taken it over, adding a few little touches of femininity to soften the strictly functional, masculine lines. Oh, nothing too frilly or trou-frou, of course—it still retained a sufficiently businesslike air.

This had used to be Adam's office. It was quite ironic, that, she reflected wryly. She had been here quite a few times when he was in occupation. She remembered herself as a coltish teenager, crazy in love, perching on the edge of his desk, laughingly teasing him to distract him from the dry old papers he was trying to concentrate on...

'He's still here, you know.'

She looked up sharply as Richard came into the room. His dark expression caused her heart to thud in panic, and in instinctive defensiveness she raised her eyebrows in innocent enquiry, as if she didn't already know exactly who he was talking about.

'Taylor,' he confirmed tersely. 'He's still hanging around. Look at this—he's demanding an extra-ordinary general meeting.' He waved the paper in his hand. 'Heaven knows what he hopes to achieve.'

'Will you agree?' she asked, her voice unsteady.

'I have no choice. I've checked it out with Gerald, and we're obliged under the articles of the company to do so.'

Tell him—tell him *now*, a voice inside her head was urging forcefully—but her courage failed her. She glanced at the letter in Richard's hand. It was on the headed notepaper of one of the most ex-clusive local hotels. 'The Pennine,' she mused, keeping her tone light. 'So that's where he's staying.' Not with Georgina?

'Apparently. Very nice for him—on our money. I hear he's bought himself a car, too—an Aston Martin, no less. That wouldn't have left him much change out of a hundred grand.'

'Really?' It was hard to inject the right amount of indifference into her voice—Richard was very astute, and he might be as suspicious if she showed too little interest as too much. 'Do you . . . do you suppose he intends to stay around for long?'

Richard shrugged. 'Who knows what he might be planning to do? My guess is that he's turned up here because it was necessary for him to clear out of Australia for a while.'

She blinked at him, puzzled. 'What do you mean?'

'Well, the way he flashes his money around . . .' He shrugged his shoulders expressively. 'We both know exactly how much income he's had from the company these past six years, and it wouldn't have supported the sort of lifestyle he seems to be accustomed to. I shouldn't be surprised to learn that he's been up to his old tricks again.'

Olivia felt suddenly cold. Of course—it made sense. He had broken into the house so easily... Was that how he could afford his expensive lifestyle? The company was doing well, but the dividend on the shares had been comfortable, rather than a fortune. And he didn't have a director's salary to supplement it, as she and Richard had.

And his charm and social position would win him invitations into some of the best houses—what a perfect opportunity for him to appraise the value of the contents, and find the weaknesses in their security...

'What was it you wanted to see me about?' Richard asked, cutting across her train of thought.

'Sorry...?'

'My secretary said you wanted to speak to me.'

'Oh...just...I wondered if we could have lunch together?' she temporised. She was going to tell him—she just needed a little more time to compose her script.

He shook his head regretfully, glancing at his wristwatch. 'Sorry—I'm having lunch with Mike Sauter, to discuss the details of this take-over.'

'Oh...' Should she tell him quickly, before he went? No—it would only be an unnecessary distraction for him, and anyway she needed time to be able to explain it all properly. 'You really think he's going to agree this time?' she asked instead.

Richard's eyes glinted with satisfaction. 'He doesn't have a lot of choice—it's that or go to the wall.'

She nodded. Sauter's had been a good firm once, but Mike's father had been an engineer, not a businessman, and he had made some serious mistakes. Since Mike had taken over the reins he had done his best to put things right, but what he needed was a substantial investment—something he was unlikely to get in the present economic climate.

He had already refused Richard's offer twice, but now it seemed that he had finally reached the end of the road, and would have to sell out. It was a shame for him, of course, to lose the firm that had been in his family for three generations—but, as Richard said, there was no room for sentiment in business.

But, even so, Adam's words had come back to whisper in her brain, reminding her of his arguments. 'By the way,' she remarked as casually as she could, 'I was looking through the figures on that deal the other night...'

Richard flickered her a warm smile. 'Burning the candle at both ends?' he teased. 'No wonder you've been looking tired.'

She shook her head. 'Oh, no, nothing like that,' she assured him quickly, hoping he wouldn't notice the slight tremor in her voice. 'But...I was just wondering... It does look as if there may have to be rather a lot of redundancies when we start to rationalise their factories...'

'But with the planned expansion in our own factories here we'll be able to offer nearly all of their employees new jobs,' he explained, his voice expressing surprise that she should not have realised that fact. 'There won't be any need for compulsory redundancies at all.'

'Oh—yes, of course.' She smiled with relief. Why had she ever doubted? She should have known that one of Richard's first concerns would be for the welfare of Sauter's workers. She should never have let Adam whisper his poisonous suspicions to her— it was part of his scheme to drive a wedge of mistrust between them.

'I'll tell you what—why don't we have dinner tonight, to celebrate?' he suggested.

She managed a smile. 'Oh, yes—that would be nice,' she agreed.

'Fine. I'll pick you up about eight o'clock, OK?' 'Fine...'

He was already gone. Aimlessly she wandered over to the window, and a few minutes later she saw him leave the building, and climb into his car, and drive away. Resolutely she sat down at her desk again, but somehow she just couldn't force her attention back to the glossy prospectus she was supposed to be studying; too many other things were troubling her mind.

Was she being selfish to want more of Richard's attention? She knew how busy he was, and yet... surely he could manage to spare her just a little more time? Maybe if he had Adam wouldn't have found her quite such easy prey. With a low moan she dropped her head into her hands. It was still humiliating to remember what had happened, the way she had responded so wantonly to his kisses, his caressing hands . . .

The insistent buzz of the telephone interrupted her thoughts, and she reached out automatically to pick it up. 'There's a caller on the line for you, Olivia,' her secretary announced, a strange note of diffidence in her voice. 'He wouldn't give his name.'

A hot little chill scudded through her—for some reason, she already knew who it was. 'Put him through, Elaine,' she requested, struggling to keep her voice level and controlled.

There was a click, and then she heard those familiar mocking tones. 'Good morning, Angel. How are you?'

'Very well, thank you,' she retorted crisply.

His soft laughter told her that he wasn't deceived for one moment by her brisk tone. 'And have you told Richard about my visit?' he taunted.

'No, I haven't.'

'Oh, naughty, naughty,' he chided her provocatively. 'Keeping secrets from your future husband, Angel? What sort of basis is that for a happy marriage?'

'I've no intention of keeping secrets from him,' she countered with dignity. 'There . . . just hasn't been time yet. He . . . he's been very busy.'

'I see.' His laughter held a low, husky note that sent a shimmer of heat down her spine. 'And what exactly will you tell him—when you finally get around to it?'

'I shall tell him everything, of course,' she responded with cold dignity.

'Everything? Like the fact that you were almost naked in my arms, that you almost let me make love to you? That your body was as hungry for mine as a desert for rain...?'

She closed her eyes, trying to shut out the images his words conjured. 'I... I'll tell him whatever's important,' she insisted weakly.

'And you don't think it's important for the poor man to know that his fiancée is on the verge of being unfaithful to him?'

'I'm not,' she protested. 'It... won't happen again.'

'Won't it?'

'I love Richard——'

'Richard's a fool,' came his voice, sensual and forceful, like his presence. 'He's taken you for granted—he should have made sure of you a long time ago. Now I'm back, and I intend to take what's mine.'

'I'm going to marry him,' she protested, her voice wavering. 'We've set the date, next month——'

'So you told me. But a lot can happen in a month.'

She closed her eyes, wishing she could stop listening to him. All she had to do was put down the telephone—why couldn't she do it?

His laughter, lazy and mocking, seemed to confirm that he knew what she was suffering. 'I'll see you at the shareholders' meeting—if not before,' he said, the faint hint of threat in his voice reminding her that even in her own home she wasn't safe from him—it seemed that he could break in any time he wanted. She would have to suggest to

Eleanor that they have the security-system seriously uprated . . .

'Oh, and by the way,' he added on an inflexion of sardonic humour, 'I hope you've got a good supply of indigestion tablets.'

'Indigestion tablets?' she repeated warily. 'Why?'

'I think you'll find Richard won't have enjoyed his lunch very much. Goodbye, Angel.'

He had hung up before she could say another word. She stared at the silent receiver, her heart pounding. The Sauter deal . . . had he found some way to sabotage it? She really should have warned Richard before he went out that Adam knew all about it . . .

She was far too much on edge to settle to any work. Restlessly she paced around her office, debating with herself whether perhaps she should follow Richard to the meeting with Mike Sauter, and warn him. But what good would that do? She had no idea what Adam was planning.

Richard's office was quite a bit larger than her own. A thick blue carpet covered the floor, and the walls were panelled in oak. It had been Lex's office before, of course, and his presence still seemed to dominate it. She couldn't help wondering . . . if Adam had become chairman, would he have been able to assert his possession more distinctly?

She sat down in the deep leather executive chair behind the desk, and gazed up at the large portrait of Lex on the wall. It had been painted in oils some twenty years before, when he was at his most formidable. That was how she remembered him—a

sometimes fierce figure, not necessarily to be
avoided, but always to be treated with caution.

Adam was the only one who had really been able
to handle him. He had usually been able to get Lex
to agree to anything he wanted—Lex could see no
wrong in him. Unbidden, her mind drifted back to
that day six years ago, when he had taken on the
daunting task of persuading Lex to let him marry
his seventeen-year-old daughter.

She had been so nervous. She had scampered into
the house and straight upstairs, afraid of bumping
into anyone, afraid that they might guess what had
just taken place. Watching anxiously from the
landing window she had seen Adam follow her up
through the garden, and then had crept back to the
top of the stairs, hiding behind the banisters, to see
him come in. What would he do?

He hadn't gone straight to Lex's study. Instead
he had gone into the drawing-room, and she had
heard the sound of the drinks cabinet being opened.
So he was nervous too, and needed a drink! She
had waited, racked with tension. Had he really
meant what he had said? Would he speak to Lex...?

She had drawn back as he came into the hall
again. He hadn't seen her... He had had a tumbler
in his hand, and he had drained its contents, putting
it down on the mahogany sideboard. And then he
had walked straight across, and knocked firmly on
Lex's door. From inside, Lex had called "Come
in"...

The murmur of voices seemed to have been going
on for an awfully long time—once or twice she

heard Lex's familiar bellow of rage. But Adam seemed to be persisting—oh, how she loved him for being so brave! After a while she decided to slip away to her room, and change her bikini for a blue and white cotton dress.

She was coming down the stairs when the study door opened, and Adam stepped out. He saw her, and smiled that smile that could set her heart soaring. 'It's all right,' he told her, holding out his hand. 'He's agreed.' She ran down to him, her feet floating on air.

Lex was sitting in the huge leather armchair in front of the marble fireplace in his study. He was always an imposing figure, with his granite-hewn features and thick white hair, but for once he was smiling—he usually only smiled like that when he had pulled off some particularly cunning business manoeuvre.

His stone-grey eyes surveyed her consideringly, but with Adam standing very close behind her, still holding her hand, she felt brave enough to return the gaze levelly. 'Well—so you want to get married, then, do you?' he demanded, his voice gruff. 'Are you absolutely sure about it?'

'Oh, yes!' she breathed, gazing up adoringly at Adam, who smiled down at her.

'Well, I suppose it's not such a bad idea,' Lex conceded, his grudging tone belied by the gleam of satisfaction in his eyes. 'With Adam controlling two thirds of the company after I'm gone, I know I won't have to worry about the future. It's a darned sight better than waiting for some damned fortune-hunter to come along and try to make a fool of you!'

She gurgled with laughter, happy that her father was so pleased with her for once.

'Mind you, my girl,' Lex went on sternly, 'you've still got your A levels to finish.'

'Oh, no!' she protested, her eyes flying to his face. 'Surely I don't have to go back to school?'

'She could finish them at the local college,' suggested Adam calmly. 'And take her business studies degree at the polytechnic. We'd like to get married as soon as possible,' he added, his voice taking on that excitingly husky timbre again.

'She's not yet eighteen,' Lex objected.

'Oh, but I will be in October,' she put in quickly.

He looked at them both, his eyebrows raised. 'October, eh? You want to rush it that soon?'

'Actually I was thinking of September,' responded Adam, squeezing her hand. 'The weather's likely to be so much more reliable then.'

Olivia felt a scarlet blush rise to her cheeks. She knew his urgency had nothing whatsoever to do with the weather...

Lex chuckled richly, understanding too. 'Damn your impudence! All right, then —September it is!'

Richard's business lunches normally went on until at least half-past two, but it was barely a quarter past one when the door of his office slammed viciously, and she heard him barking at his secretary. She jumped to her feet, her heart in her mouth, as the connecting door opened.

'What's wrong?' she asked tautly. 'What's happened?'

'He's pulled out! Just like that—right at the last minute!'

'But . . . How could he? He's on the verge of bankruptcy——'

'He's found a backer. Someone he's "not at liberty to name", if you please!' He swung back into his own office, and went straight over to the hospitality bar, pouring himself what looked like a very generous slug of scotch. 'Apparently this mysterious Sir Galahad has offered to be a sleeping partner, leaving Sauter with an option to buy him out again in five years.'

Olivia frowned, puzzled. 'That sounds almost too good to be true . . .' How on earth had Adam been able to pull together the finance to back such a deal, in so short a time? 'Of course, it would be just what Mike would want—it sounds as if it leaves him with total control.'

'Of course it does. And it *is* too good to be true— no sensible businessman would offer a deal like that!'

'Have you . . . any idea who it is?' she enquired, almost biting her tongue as her conscience stabbed her for not telling Richard the truth.

He tossed off his drink, and poured himself another. 'There's only one person it could be!' he asserted bitterly. 'This is his way of getting at me— he's willing to waste thousands on propping up a failing company, just to thwart my plans.'

She sat down on one of the chairs beside his desk—she didn't feel strong enough to go on standing. 'But I don't understand,' she protested, frowning as she looked up at him. 'Why should he hate *you* so much?'

Richard laughed with a touch of asperity. 'Because I've got the one thing that he really wants...'

She breathed in sharply. 'Control of the company.'

The company—always the company! Just for a fleeting moment, Olivia felt a stab of impatience. Didn't it even occur to him that Adam might want *her*, too? But the next instant she suppressed the thought. The main reason Adam wanted her was for her shares in the company. And of course Richard would never suspect her of being disloyal to him—he believed he could trust her.

'What I'd like to know,' Richard was continuing, his face grim, 'is where he got his information from. How did he know I was moving on Sauter's? There must have been a leak from somewhere inside this company, and when I find out who it is...'

His fist clenched, and Olivia swallowed hard. She really ought to tell him now—but when he was in this frame of mind... Maybe it would be better to wait until he'd cooled off a bit. Then she'd tell him. She couldn't go on keeping him in the dark—it wasn't fair.

He moved over to his desk, and sat down. 'Well, he needn't think he's got the better of me,' he vowed grimly. 'In fact, he's made a big mistake, tying himself up with Sauter like that. They aren't the only company around here worth dealing with.

He'll soon find I can move a darned sight quicker than he can.'

He seemed ready to bury himself in his papers again at once, and she stood looking at him uncertainly, reluctant to disturb him. But he glanced up, and a frown crossed his face. 'Oh...I'd promised to take you out to dinner tonight, hadn't I?' he reminded himself.

'It doesn't matter,' she assured him quickly, taking her cue from the faint shadow of impatience in his voice.

He looked relieved. 'You don't mind?' He reached for her hand, and gave it an apologetic squeeze. 'I'm really sorry, darling, but you can see how it is.' His glance indicated his cluttered desk. 'We'll make it another time.'

'Yes, of course.' She fought to hide her disappointment. After all, it wasn't Richard's fault, what had happened, and it had made a great deal of extra work for him. 'Well, I...I'd better not interrupt you any longer. Anyway, I've a lot on myself this afternoon.'

'Fine...'

Already he was absorbed in what he was doing, and she retreated to her own office, closing the door carefully behind her. She was aware that she was shaking, and crossed quickly to her desk, sitting down in the deep leather executive chair.

So Adam had made his first move. The level of his spite almost took her breath away—if Sauter's failed to turn the corner, he could be throwing away a fortune! And meanwhile, of course, Richard could pursue other projects—as he had said, there were plenty of other companies ripe for a take-over. But it wouldn't be the same. Damn Adam Taylor!

'He's doing this deliberately. He thinks he can make me lose my nerve.'

Olivia glanced anxiously at Richard. The whiteness of tension around his mouth betrayed the fact that, whatever he said, it *was* getting to him the way Adam had been dogging their footsteps these past ten days. Of course it could be argued that it was the most natural thing in the world for him to show up at an engineering trades exhibition—after all, he was an engineer by qualification. But it didn't *feel* like a coincidence.

'How the hell did he know we were going to be here?' Richard demanded in a taut undervoice. 'Is he psychic?'

Was it her imagination, or was he looking at her with a shade of suspicion? She knew—only too well—how Adam had come by so much detailed knowledge about their plans; he must have checked her diary at the same time as he had broken into the safe. The guilty secret was gnawing at her conscience.

But Richard had been so furious about the supposed leak, throwing the whole company into a furore of whispering and suspicion before she had had a chance to say anything, that she hadn't been able to bring herself to confess what had really occured.

'Perhaps he's just come to see the exhibition?' she suggested, knowing that her voice didn't sound very steady.

'Hmph! And pigs might fly,' snorted Richard in derision. 'And what's he doing with Jim Marston's daughter? That's what I'd like to know. Jim's one of our best customers—if he's planning to put a spoke in there . . .! Look out, he's coming over,' he added swiftly, turning away from the front of their stand to find an outlet for his ire in bawling out a couple of the sales-team for the untidiness of one of the displays.

His warning had been unnecessary—Olivia was already far too acutely aware of Adam's approach. She recognised the tall blonde at his side, too. She had known Joanna Marston for a long time, though not very well; she had certainly never had any reason to dislike her. But what she felt right now wasn't really dislike, she was forced to admit to herself. It was jealousy.

Her heart-rate had accelerated uncomfortably, and it took a great deal of self-control to maintain her cool façade. He had paused beside the next stand, and was chatting with casual unconcern to some acquaintances, as if he wasn't even aware of her presence.

For a moment she wondered if she could find some excuse to escape until he had gone, but that would look far too obvious—both to him and to Richard. No—she would just have to brazen it out. One of the things that Lex had taught her was that in business it could be useful to cultivate a poker-face and not show what you were thinking, and she was grateful for that skill now.

His conversation over, Adam had drawn level with their stand, pausing to survey it with an air of interest and approval that Olivia did not trust at all. Then his eyes fell on the two of them, and a faintly sardonic smile curved that hard mouth.

'Richard, Olivia– what a pleasant surprise,' he drawled, knowing that they knew it was nothing of the sort. 'I believe you must know Richard and Olivia, Joanna?'

'Of course.' Joanna Marston smiled a little uncertainly, clearly sensing the undercurrents of tension that were in the air. 'How are you?'

Adam glanced around the vast hangar-like exhibition hall, crowded with gloomy trade stands and thronging with people. 'This affair has grown quite considerably since I was last here,' he remarked, clearly indifferent to any embarrassment at referring to his extended absence from the locality. 'By the way, Ricky, I assume I'll be hearing from you within the next few days regarding the extraordinary meeting I requested?'

'Naturally.' Richard had stiffened at his use of that juvenile shortening of his name, especially in front of several of his interested employees. 'Your requisition was in order, and you'll be receiving a response in due course, in accordance with the articles of the company.'

'Good.' His eyes glinted with mocking humour at Richard's pompous speech. 'Well, I look forward to that, then.' He put his hand on Joanna's elbow, and together they walked away; they looked good together, Olivia acknowledged bitterly. Was that the way the wind was blowing?

CHAPTER FIVE

THE large oval table in the boardroom of Lambert, Taylor & Simpson had been buffed to a gleaming mahogany, and laid out with leather-bound blotters bearing the company's logo. Four places had been set—for the first time ever the four shareholders were to meet together formally.

Olivia glanced anxiously at her watch. Five minutes to ten—Adam would be here at any minute. It was all very proper, and—on the surface—quite innocuous. He had put forward a resolution—as he was perfectly entitled to do as a shareholder—calling for the cancellation of Richard's plans to close one of their subsidiary factories. But he knew he would automatically be out-voted—so what was his real motive in calling for the meeting?

She had been living on a knife-edge these past two weeks, as Richard had grown more and more angry about the "leak". He had even talked of bringing in the police. If only she had told him straight away—it would have been so much easier. Now, with every day that had passed, it had become harder and harder to confess.

But somehow she was going to have to find the courage—she couldn't go on like this. She hadn't even been able to eat properly, and at the last fitting her wedding-dress had had to be taken in by more than an inch. The fear that Adam was going to spill the beans had been keeping her awake at night ...

She was so tense that she started as the door opened. It was Richard; he cast a look of irritable resentment at the fourth place at the table as he crossed the room and took his place in the chairman's seat. 'Well—so we're to be honoured today,' he remarked tautly. 'I don't know why he's bothering to waste his time—or ours.'

Olivia moved over and sat down in the chair to his right—her usual place at their monthly board-meetings. Georgina usually sat opposite her. She was nominally a director, but her attendance at meetings was at best erratic and rarely very constructive; her father had known that, which was why he'd given Richard the larger portion of his own third of the shares, and Georgina only ten per cent. Most meetings were really little more than a formality—she and Richard didn't need a monthly meeting to discuss and agree on their plans.

'Still, it may turn out to our advantage after all,' Richard went on, his smile grim. 'I'd very much like a chance to find out what his next move is going to be. I might be able to get him to let something slip.'

Olivia picked up her slim gold pen, and twirled it nervously in her fingers. Personally she doubted very much that Adam would let slip anything he didn't intend to. It was what he might *intend* to let slip that was worrying her. Drawing a deep breath, she steeled herself to speak. But before she could open her mouth there was a light tap on the door, and Richard's secretary appeared.

'Mr Taylor and Mrs Collins have just driven on to the car park, sir,' she reported, her calm professional façade not quite hiding the suppressed excitement that had been fizzing through the whole building since the news had leaked out that Adam was going to be putting in an appearance—and she had never even met him!

'Thank you, Maureen,' Richard responded, his voice so totally normal that even Olivia might have been deceived if she hadn't known the truth. 'Bring them in as soon as they come up, please.'

The girl nodded, a little dampened, and withdrew.

'Richard...'

'Jim Marston was on the phone earlier,' he cut across her, so wound up in his own worries that he hadn't even heard her tentative beginning. 'He doesn't like the latest price increases on the diamond reamers.'

'Nobody likes price increases,' Olivia responded quickly. 'Richard, about——'

'I've a feeling Taylor's planning to undercut us, using Sauter's. If that's his idea of loyalty, after all these years—the firm his own father helped to found...!'

'Richard, about the leak.' Her voice was urgent—this could be her last chance, and at last she succeeded in catching his attention. 'There wasn't a leak. Adam... got the information out of my safe.'

He frowned at her, puzzled. 'But... What are you talking about, Olivia?' he asked sharply. 'How?'

'He broke into the house one night, and cracked the safe open...'

'He *what*?'

'I found him in the study in the middle of the night, reading my papers,' she explained. Her hands were shaking, the blood was throbbing in her temples. 'I... I didn't call the police, because... I thought... well, we wouldn't really want that sort of publicity...'

He was staring at her in blank astonishment. 'But why didn't you tell *me*?' he demanded. 'You let me go on thinking...' His eyes narrowed. 'What else happened?'

'Nothing!'

'Then why didn't you tell me about it?'

'I was going to,' she stammered, unable to look at him. 'But... I was afraid you would be angry...'

'*Angry*?' He certainly was. 'Don't you think——?'

The door opened without a knock, and Richard's secretary, pent-up with anticipation, ushered in the two other players in the game. Caught in the middle of their quarrel, Olivia and Richard both looked up sharply, neither of them able to hide the tension that was arcing between them.

Georgina was wearing a black leather mini-skirt, so tight that it was a puzzle how she could walk in it, and a black lace bustier that looked as if it had come straight out of a tart's underwear drawer— strange attire for a formal business-meeting, perhaps, but no surprise to those who knew her. She favoured her brother with a sarcastic smile, and took her place, pushing her chair well back from the table so that she could lounge in it comfortably.

Olivia couldn't prevent herself from flashing the older woman a look of scorn—she seemed to be trying to look as young as her own teenage daughter, and not succeeding at all. But her eyes were drawn inevitably to the man who had followed her into the room.

He was wearing a light grey business suit, the jacket moulded to his wide shoulders by the hand of an expert—and undoubtedly expensive—tailor. That all too familiar sardonic smile had curved his hard mouth as he glanced from Olivia to Richard, and back again.

'I'm sorry,' he drawled, just enough mockery in his voice to sting. 'Did we come in at the wrong moment?'

There was a silence like a four-minute warning. Richard had half risen to his feet, his fists clenched, but Olivia put a restraining hand on his arm, urging him back into his seat. Adam's dark eyes glinted with satisfaction; he had them all dancing like puppets on his string.

He sat down in the fourth place—even that action seemed loaded, as if he was reminding them that his rightful place was at the head of the table—and the expression of mocking expectancy on his face as he looked towards Richard was a further deliberate goad.

But Richard had himself well under control now. 'Shall we begin the meeting?' he suggested blandly, glancing down at the paper in front of him. 'There's only one resolution on the agenda.'

At his side, his secretary was poised with her pen and shorthand notebook, her chair pushed back just a little further from the table than usual, her legs crossed with a self-conscious elegance that Olivia knew was for Adam's benefit—and the faintly sardonic smile on his face confirmed that he was fully aware of that too.

She slanted him a look of icy disdain, but his eyes merely flickered with amusement, and she looked away again, angry at his arrogant assumption that she was jealous. It wasn't that at all—it was simply that . . . some kinds of behaviour were just not appropriate in the boardroom.

With an effort of will she tried to force her attention back to the business of the meeting, but it wasn't easy to concentrate. Across the table, she could sense Adam watching her, as if he could see right through her mask of cool composure and know every thought that was going through her mind. It really shouldn't be like this, she told herself, feeling a kind of panic starting inside her. She shouldn't be so constantly aware of him, he shouldn't have such a powerful effect on her...

'. . . and I'm quite sure Olivia will agree with me on that, won't you, darling?'

She jerked herself sharply back to reality as Richard touched her hand. She hadn't even heard what he had said—but she knew he was expecting her to support him, so she nodded. 'Oh, yes—of course. Absolutely.'

'Really?' Adam slanted her a look laced with contempt. 'I'm surprised to hear that you should share that opinion.'

She felt her cheeks tinge faintly with pink. What had she said she agreed with?

'You can't make an omelette without breaking a few eggs,' Richard retorted. 'Those of the work-force that could be re-deployed to the factory here...'

Olivia swiftly realised what they had been talking about, but she bit back the protest she had been about to utter. She *didn't* fully agree with Richard over his decision to close the factory, mainly be-cause of the effect it would have on the workforce in an area where unemployment was still high. But she wouldn't say so in front of Adam.

Adam was shaking his head. 'It's a long way to travel into Derby,' he pointed out. 'Especially for those who haven't got cars.'

'Then let them move closer!'

'That's not so easy as you appear to think. Homes in this area are quite a bit more expensive, and a lot of the unskilled workforce would probably be council tenants anyway.'

'We're running a business here, not a damned charity!' Richard exploded.

'Strangely enough, it can be possible—and in the long run more profitable—to make the welfare of your employees one of your main priorities,' Adam remarked in a sardonic drawl. 'That was a prin-ciple that even a few of the more enlightened Victorian industrialists realised. Lex understood it— it's a shame you didn't try to learn a little more from him while you had the chance.'

'I could hardly get near him, with you sucking up to him all the time,' Richard threw back, his words laced with a bitterness that took Olivia by surprise.

Adam lifted one dark eyebrow in cool enquiry. 'Is that so?' he responded with mocking interest. 'Well, now—perhaps the truth is finally coming out. Perhaps you've hated me all along, for always beating you into second place. Is that how it's been?'

Olivia stared from him to Richard, confused by this unexpected twist. It wasn't true—Richard had genuinely admired Adam, had never resented his successes. Even after Adam had been arrested, it had been a very long time before Richard had come to accept that he was guilty of what they said he had done.

Richard was struggling to regain control of himself—the effort it was costing him showed in his face. But then he smiled, dismissing Adam's accusation with a gesture of his hand. 'What you can't accept is that it's *me* who controls the company now,' he retaliated forcefully. 'Whether you like it or not, we're going ahead with our plans, and there's not a damned thing you can do about it.'

'No?' Adam lifted a sardonic eyebrow. 'I think you'll find I can still put a spoke in your wheel.'

'Empty threats!' mocked Richard, sneering. 'You don't impress me.'

Adam laughed again, and rose to his feet. 'Oh, I don't make empty threats,' he advised, an unmistakable message of warning in his voice. 'You'll find that out soon enough. Coming, Georgie?'

Georgina stood up, teetering on her impossibly high stiletto heels. 'You might as well save your energy,' she recommended to her brother. 'You won't beat him—he's a hundred times cleverer than you.' And, with a triumphant glance at Olivia, she followed him from the room.

There was a long, long moment of silence. Olivia glanced anxiously at Richard, aware that his secretary was still sitting there listening with discreet interest to everything that was going on. There was no reason to doubt her confidentiality about anything to do with the company, but she might not be above sharing the odd titbit of personal gossip with the other senior secretaries over lunch.

Richard had evidently had the same thought, because he forced himself to smile, and said calmly, 'Well, we knew that would be a waste of time, didn't we? There seems little point in continuing with the meeting now, so I propose that we formally adjourn it.'

Olivia nodded agreement with a sense of relief. She had been dreading this meeting, and now at least it was over. Of course there was still the matter of the break-in, a bone of contention between her and Richard—and she knew that he hadn't forgotten it. But by mutual agreement they waited until they were alone in his office to raise the matter again.

He sat down at his desk, and his smile was a little thin as he looked up at her—and she couldn't help noticing the strained look in his eyes. 'All right— there seems little point in crying over spilt milk,' he conceded wryly. 'You didn't tell me about the break-in, and that's it. But, from now on, let's be completely honest with each other.' He reached out and took her hand gently in his. 'Nothing would please Taylor more than if he could split us up,' he reminded her, his grey eyes serious. 'And I, for one, don't intend to let him do that.'

'Nor do I,' she vowed, returning his smile with warm affection. 'I'm sorry, Richard. I should have told you.'

'Well, we won't talk about it any more,' he promised. 'The thing to do now is to try to limit the damage.' He cast a jaded eye over the piles of paper on his desk. 'It looks as if I'm going to be kept pretty busy. And if he's going to try to stop us closing the Workoop factory I'd better take another look at our plans, and make sure there are no loopholes he can use.'

He seemed ready to bury himself in his work again, and Olivia hesitated, reluctant to distract him. 'You...won't forget it's Felicity's dinner party tomorrow night?' she reminded him diffidently.

He frowned with a touch of impatience—clearly he *had* forgotten. 'Tomorrow? Oh, dear... I'm not at all sure that I'm going to be able to make it.' He reached for her hand, and gave it an affectionate squeeze. 'I'm really sorry, darling. But you can make my excuse for me, can't you?'

'Yes, of course.' She forced herself to hide her disappointment. How many times had it happened like this, that she had had to cry off an invitation at the last minute, or go on her own, because something serious had cropped up that demanded Richard's immediate attention?

He lifted her hand to his lips, and kissed the backs of her fingers. 'But don't worry—I shall make sure my desk is absolutely clear by next weekend,' he promised sincerely. 'I've no intention of taking work with me on our honeymoon!'

She returned his smile rather weakly. Only just over a week . . . it was coming around so quickly . . . She ought to be getting excited by now, but she felt only a kind of hollow emptiness . . . Oh, it was probably only pre-wedding nerves, she scolded herself briskly. Richard was probably feeling exactly the same.

She glanced down at his light brown head, already bent over his work. She really shouldn't be cross with him for ducking out of Fliss's dinner party. After all, he was doing it for both of them, for the company. Richard took his responsibilities very seriously.

It was unfair of Adam to imply that Richard didn't care for their employees—he cared very much. But he knew that to keep the company viable in difficult economic times it was sometimes necessary to make hard decisions. It was doubtful that Adam could have made a better job of it if he had been chairman.

Fliss and Donald Parker were an American couple, who had moved into the county a little over a year ago when Donald had taken up an appointment as a senior consultant surgeon at the local hospital. Olivia had met Fliss through a committee that was raising funds for a new cobalt unit at the hospital—

Fliss was a formidable fund-raiser—and the two had struck up an immediate friendship.

It was a little after eight o'clock when she parked the XJS in the long drive of the Parkers' pleasant, rambling house on the outskirts of town. A number of other cars were already there, and she recognised most of them, so she wasn't too apprehensive about going in on her own.

It was just rather awkward, having to explain Richard's absence yet again. Fliss had been very understanding on the telephone, and had assured her that it wouldn't upset her arrangements at all, but no hostess liked to find herself suddenly one guest short around her dinner table.

Fliss came to answer the door herself. 'Hi!' That wide smile of welcome would have made anyone feel at ease. 'Come on in.' She reached out an eager hand, and drew her into the hall.

'I'm sorry I'm a bit late,' Olivia responded, slipping off her silk jacket and giving it to her friend to hang up in the small cloakroom beside the door. 'Am I the last?'

'Yes—but it's OK, we weren't ready to sit down yet anyway.'

'I'm sorry about Richard,' added Olivia wryly. 'He really would have come if he possibly could, but something came up at the last minute...'

Fliss smiled. 'Oh, it doesn't matter—if he couldn't come, he couldn't come. Besides, I managed to get a spare man at the last moment,' she added, linking her arm cosily through Olivia's as they walked through to the charming sitting-room at the back of the house, where the other guests were gathered. 'You must come and meet him. He's absolutely charming—and so generous! Carol Sauter introduced me to him—apparently he's some kind of business-partner of her husband's. So of course—you know me!—I asked him if he'd donate a prize for our raffle, and right away he said he would.'

There were a dozen people in the room, but Olivia saw only one. For one desperate moment she felt a powerful desire to run away, but already he had seen her, and that sardonic smile confirmed that he wasn't in the least surprised to see her here. Her diary again, she surmised bitterly.

Fliss waved to him, totally unaware that at her side Olivia had stiffened. 'Adam! Hey, come on over here and say hello to another one of our committee. Olivia, this is Adam Taylor. As I was saying, he's been most amazingly generous—he's offered to give us a whole crate of champagne as a raffle prize!'

'Has he? How kind!' Her voice was laden with saccharin, but the message of her eyes was ice-cold. Once again he had managed to manipulate the situation to suit himself. But why had he gone to so much trouble to get himself an invitation to Fliss's dinner party? What devil's plot was he hatching now?

His dark eyes flickered with mocking amusement, quite aware of her displeasure, and then he let them drift over her in an insolent appraisal, as if he was visualising the naked curves beneath the smoke-coloured silk dress—curves that his smile reminded her he was a good deal more familiar with than he ought to be.

'Ah, Olivia and I already know each other very well, Fliss,' he drawled smoothly. 'As a matter of fact we were once engaged to be married.'

'Oh...!' Poor Fliss paled in distress—unknowingly she had committed one of the most dreaded *faux pas* of the social hostess. 'I...I'm sorry...I didn't know...'

'Oh, it's quite all right,' he assured her, all urbane charm. 'It was a very long time ago, and we're good friends again now—aren't we, Angel?'

'Yes.' She almost bit the word out, but she had no choice other than to agree—her friend would be so upset if she knew the truth. 'Yes, of course.'

'Oh...good...' Fliss sounded only half convinced. 'Well, I er—I think perhaps we could go in to dinner now, if everyone's ready? Donald?' She grabbed at her husband's elbow in relief, and led the way through into the spacious dining-room, aglow with candles and crystal glasses, and highly polished silverware. 'Just sit wherever you want to, everyone,' she invited, spreading her arms. 'We don't want to be formal, do we?'

Adam had followed Olivia closely, and she looked around desperately for a way to avoid being seated next to him. But as he drew out a chair for her she knew that she was trapped. Everyone else was already settling themselves, and to have refused to sit beside him would have created an awkward scene. Reluctantly she took the place, and picked up her linen napkin, unfolding it on to her lap.

'What a pleasant occasion,' remarked Adam, deliberately provocative. 'Such a pity that Richard couldn't be here.'

'He was very busy,' she retorted stiffly—she hadn't forgotten that it was Adam's interference that had made so much extra work for him.

He laughed softly. 'Even so, it's a little...reckless of him, to let you come alone,' he taunted, his dark gaze lingering around her again, making her realise how inadequate her defences were against him. 'Does he always take so little care of you? Isn't he afraid that some big bad wolf might come along and steal you away?'

His low, husky words brought a flame of colour to her cheeks. 'Richard knows that he can trust me,' she countered, trying to inject a frosty rejection into her voice.

'Does he indeed?'

'And, in case you're wondering, I have told him about the way you broke into the house,' she added with lofty disdain.

He laughed softly. 'Oh, have you? And did you tell him what happened?' he taunted. 'He seems to have taken it all remarkably well. If our positions had been reversed, I'd have been round to see me right away, and it wouldn't have been a rational adult discussion I'd have been looking for.'

She let her soft mouth curl into a faint sneer. 'But then Richard isn't the kind to behave like that,' she responded coolly. 'He doesn't need to talk with his fists.'

'That's probably just as well.'

She felt her fingers clench in anger around the handle of her fork—she would have loved to have poked the sharp prongs right into his mocking eyes. With a struggle she forced herself to concentrate all her attention on the ceviche of Dover sole that Fliss had so painstakingly prepared for their starter—she had to regain some semblance of composure before anyone should notice how agitated she was.

'Apparently the information you found out about the Sauter deal was useful to you, anyway,' she slanted at him tautly.

That sardonic smile curved his hard mouth. 'Extremely,' he confirmed with mocking satisfaction. 'Was poor Richard terribly disappointed?'

'Naturally he wasn't very pleased,' she admitted—she could hardly deny it. Her eyes searched his face. 'Why do you hate him so much?' she asked, almost wearily. 'What did he ever do to you?'

There was no reading the enigmatic glint in those dark eyes. 'Let's just say that I have my reasons. But in this instance I was concerned only to help an old friend, and keep a good company from being destroyed.'

'Richard wasn't going to destroy it—he was going to save it!' Suddenly she realised that her protest had been a little too loud, falling into a lull in the conversation, and one or two people had glanced towards her in curiosity. She subsided, embarrassed, furious with Adam for being the cause of her discomfiture. 'Of course it would have been necessary to restructure a little——'

'Restructure?' He lifted one dark eyebrow in sardonic enquiry. 'You know, you're even beginning to *sound* like him. But I suppose that's hardly surprising—he wouldn't want to risk letting you think for yourself, would he?'

She slanted him a look of calculated hauteur. 'I don't know what you mean,' she countered coldly.

'He was so concerned for you after I was arrested, wasn't he? Good old Richard, the brick, the shoulder to cry on.' The sneer in his voice stung. 'He spun his spider-web around you, and you didn't even realise.'

Olivia had tried to close her ears, refusing to listen to his insidious persuasion. Richard *had* been very kind to her—she didn't know what she would have done without him, with Lex in hospital and all her tender young dreams in ruins. She wasn't going to let Adam twist that around into something evil, calculated.

Fliss was watching her, still anxiously doubting her insistence that there was nothing wrong, and she made herself smile, as if she was enjoying herself. But it was impossible to do justice to Fliss's delicious cooking, and she couldn't even escape by turning to her other neighbour for conversation— his young wife, heavily pregnant, was sitting beside him and absorbing all his attention.

After dinner they lingered around the table, drinking coffee. Most of the guests were associated with Fliss's fund-raising efforts in one way or another, and they spent a long time chatting, chewing over new money-making ideas.

It was a relief to Olivia when at last the evening came to an end, and she was able to escape to the kitchen on the pretext of helping to clear up. 'Well, I think that went off quite well, don't you?' asked Fliss cheerfully as she loaded the dishwasher. 'There—the miracles of modern technology.' She closed the door with a sigh of satisfaction. 'We can just leave it to get on with it. Would you like another coffee?'

'I wouldn't mind,' agreed Olivia, smiling. She had planned to linger as long as she politely could, to ensure that Adam was well away from the vicinity before she left the house.

Her friend slanted her a look of interested enquiry. 'I'm sorry if I made it awkward for you tonight,' she said. 'I had no idea you even knew him. Was he the "Taylor" in Lambert, Taylor & Simpson?'

'Originally his father was,' Olivia confirmed, keeping her tone light as she nibbled one of the left-over after-dinner mints. 'His parents were killed quite a few years ago, and he inherited a third of the company.' She hesitated. 'I suppose I'd better tell you, before you hear it from anyone else——'

'About him going to prison?' Fliss interrupted, smiling. 'Yes, I know—he told me.'

'He *told* you?'

'Yes. But I take people as I find them, and I've found him to be perfectly charming.'

'You don't wonder where he got the money from to pay for that very generous crate of champagne?' asked Olivia drily.

Fliss giggled. 'Lord—do you think it's hot?' she asked. 'I don't mean hot champagne—that wouldn't be very nice. But...'

'I know what you mean,' returned Olivia, shocked.

Fliss's eyes were dancing, but her voice was serious. 'I really don't think so,' she insisted. 'He told me it was all a mistake—he wasn't guilty.'

Olivia laughed drily. 'But then he would say that, wouldn't he?' she pointed out.

'Well, I believe him.' Her eyes lit with curiosity. 'Is that why you broke off your engagement with him?' she enquired. 'When he went to prison?'

'Yes.' Olivia felt uncomfortable—for the first time, she was aware of a fundamental difference of opinion with her friend.

Fliss's mouth twisted into a wry smile. 'Well, I won't say anything,' she said, though her eyes were speaking volumes. 'It's your business.'

They drank their coffee, idly gossiping about mutual friends and finishing up a few of the left-overs. After a while Donald wandered in to join them, beaming with self-satisfaction for having done his share of the chores by vacuuming the dining-room carpet.

'Big deal,' his wife teased him. 'Apart from taking the cellophane off the box of After-Eight mints, that's been your only contribution to the entire evening!'

'I provided my charming presence,' he protested, slipping his arm around her and giving her a squeeze. 'Wasn't that enough for you?'

'Egotist!' She punched him lightly on the shoulder.

'Pugilist!' he countered, picking her up and whirling her round, depositing her on the draining-board.

Olivia watched them, slightly wistful. They had such a good marriage—could her marriage to Richard ever be as good as that? She knew that Fliss wouldn't have dreamed of expecting Donald to help with the preparations for the party—for one thing he had had a very busy day, only arriving home twenty minutes ahead of the first guest, and besides she enjoyed it all herself far too much to let anyone interfere.

'Well, I think I'd better be going,' she suggested, glancing at her wristwatch. 'Thank you for a lovely dinner.'

'Goodnight.' Donald dropped an affectionate kiss on her cheek. 'Mind how you drive home.'

Fliss walked out to the hall with her, and brought her jacket out of the cloakroom. 'I'll see you next week, then,' she said. 'We've got some great prizes for the raffle—now we'll just have to see if we can get the tickets printed for nothing!'

Olivia laughed. 'I'm sure you will!' she asserted as she waved goodbye.

CHAPTER SIX

OLIVIA'S car was the only one left on the drive now, and she let herself into it, and turned the key confidently in the ignition. Nothing happened. Puzzled, she tried again—she had never had a problem like this with it before. The engine was completely dead.

Her heart gave a thud of alarm as the door beside her opened. 'Got a problem?' enquired Adam—the note of mild amusement in his voice convinced her that it was no coincidence that he was still here.

'It won't start,' she told him, her eyes searching his face for some clue to confirm that he had actually been tinkering with her car.

'Oh, dear. Would you like me to try it?' he enquired with a concern that was transparently counterfeit.

'I don't suppose there's much point,' she responded frostily, letting him know that she knew what he'd done.

'What's the matter?' Fliss had been watching from the front door, and now she came down the drive to investigate.

Olivia quickly pinned a smile in place. 'My car won't start,' she explained with just the right degree of weary resignation.

Adam promptly stepped in with the offer she had been expecting. 'I'll run you home.'

'Oh, I wouldn't dream of putting you to so much trouble,' she responded in saccharin tones, slanting him a look of cool disdain that Fliss wouldn't see. 'I can call the RAC.'

'But they could take an hour or more to get here, and there's no guarantee that they could fix it,' he pointed out, his dark eyes giving notice that he intended to get his own way. 'It would be far easier to get a garage to come out in the morning, and tow it in. And besides,' he added with a smile of malicious triumph, 'you don't want to make Fliss and Donald wait up any longer, do you?'

That was his trump card, and he knew it. Already Fliss was looking worried, wondering why she should be so reluctant to accept his help if, as he had claimed, they were good friends. 'Very well,' she agreed with a curdled smile. 'Thank you very much.'

'It was a good job I didn't drive off straight away,' he remarked for Fliss's benefit as he took her arm.

'Wasn't it just?' she responded acidly. Her eyes flickered over the sleek grey Aston Martin parked in the kerb. 'This is yours?' she enquired.

'Do you like it?'

'Oh, it's beautiful,' she conceded drily, as he held open the door for her.

He chuckled softly, but didn't say anything more. She watched him warily as he walked round and slid into the driver's seat beside her. What was he planning? He had gone to quite a lot of trouble to manoeuvre her into this situation. It was absolutely vital that she remain cool.

But as he reached the top of the road she realised that he was intending to turn left instead of right. 'Where are you going?' she demanded, her voice rising in agitation. 'Take me home.'

'Later,' he insisted on a note of firm intent. 'First there's something I'd like you to see.'

'What?'

'Let's just say it's something that may be of interest to you,' he responded mysteriously. 'Of course, you may know all about it already, in which case I shall apologise for wasting your time.'

'What are you talking about?' she protested, filling her voice with anger to disguise the panic she was feeling. 'There's absolutely nothing that *you* could show me that would be of any interest to me whatsoever.'

'We'll see,' he countered, maddeningly indifferent to any arrows she could fire at him. 'It won't take very long.'

She sat back in her seat, staring grimly out of the side-window, fuelling her anger by reciting a mental litany of all the things he had done since he had returned to England. But in the confined space of the car she was all too vividly aware of that powerful male presence, and she couldn't deny that he made her feel more exquisitely feminine than she could recall feeling with anyone else.

It was with something of a surprise that she realised that they were driving over to Nottingham, and even more of a surprise when they turned down into one of the least salubrious quarters of the town. 'Where on earth are we going?' she enquired, peering up at the tall, dilapidated warehouses on each side of the road.

He flickered her an enigmatic smile. 'Never been here before?'

'No, I haven't—and I'm not at all sure I want to be here now,' she retorted tartly.

'Don't worry,' he reassured her laconically. 'I'll take care of you.'

He turned left through a narrow entrance, into a cobbled yard surrounded by high, blank walls, and parked the car. Somewhat to her surprise, Olivia realised that the Lagonda was not going to look at all conspicuous among the BMWs and Porsches already there.

'Well, if you don't mind risking parking your car here . . .' she remarked tartly, releasing her seatbelt and opening her own door before he could come round and help her.

He laughed drily. 'Oh, it'll be safe enough—the security around here may be unconventional, but it's effective.'

For the first time she noticed shadows lurking in the darkness, faces she couldn't see. A shiver of fear ran through her. Where had he brought her—and why? But she wasn't going to let him see her fear. She turned to him, her eyes ice-cold. 'All right, we're here,' she said. 'Now would you mind telling me what all this is about?'

'Come inside,' he responded, taking her arm. 'And mind how you walk—the ground's a bit rough, and I wouldn't want you to twist your ankle. Though I might enjoy it if I had to carry you,' he added with a wicked smile.

Angry, wishing she had firmly refused to even get into his car in the first place, she shook off his arm and stalked ahead of him...at least for several steps. But the cobbled ground was extremely difficult to walk on in high heels, and after nearly toppling in a most undignified manner she was forced to concede.

They came to a heavy wooden door, reached by descending three stone steps. Adam held it open for her, and she stepped rather nervously inside, to find herself in an opulent reception area. The walls were lined with quilted panels of red velvet, and the carpet beneath her feet was thick and luxurious.

As she gazed around, startled and confused, a huge man, taller even than Adam, appeared through the far door. His nose was crumpled, and the tailored formality of his evening clothes did nothing to disguise the bearing and physique of a street-fighter.

His shrewd eyes studied Adam with a professional suspicion that carried a hint of warning. 'You're not a member, sir?' he asked—a politely rhetorical question.

Adam shook his head. 'My name's Taylor,' he said. 'Harry's expecting us.'

To judge from the change of expression on the big man's face, that name carried considerable weight around here. 'Of course, sir,' he said, beaming. 'Mr Scott told me you'd be in tonight. If you would just step this way?'

He opened a door that had been concealed within the panelling of the wall, and stood aside to invite them to pass through. They climbed a narrow staircase, and came to a small, dimly lit landing, with one door. The bruiser tapped on it lightly, and a voice from inside called, 'Come in.'

As the bruiser opened the door, Olivia hesitated, her mouth dry, her palms moist. Whatever it was that Adam had wanted to show her, she was about to find out.

She found herself in a large, low-ceilinged room, lit by several silk-shaded lamps that spilled a soft red glow. To one side stood a massive mahogany desk, and behind it an old-fashioned green safe with a brass wheel for a handle. An expensive Aubusson carpet covered the floor. On the far side was a small but very well-stocked bar.

There were only two people in the room. At the sight of Adam, the older of them rose to his feet, coming over to greet him with all the spontaneous warmth of old friendship. 'Adam! Good to see you—it's been a long, long time. What will you have to drink?'

Olivia studied him warily. Like the man who had shown them in, he wore a dinner-jacket, its expensive tailoring a sharp contrast to his rough-edged accent. She judged him to be about fifty, with a lean, clever face—and the most cynical eyes she had ever seen.

How did Adam come to know a man like this? As they shook hands, she sensed a mutual respect between them. Had they met in prison? It was natural, perhaps, that Adam would have formed some associations there with people he would never normally have met, but she was surprised that he should have chosen to continue them so many years later.

He drew her forward, introducing her as formally as if they were at some society cocktail party. 'Angel, I'd like you to meet a very good friend of mine,' he said. 'Harry Scott.'

'So you're Angel.' He smiled at her, surveying her with the slightly wistful admiration of a man who was wishing he was twenty years younger. 'I've heard a great deal about you. Adam and I—er—shared a suite at one of Her Majesty's less salubrious establishments a few years ago.'

'How do you do?' she murmured, falling back on the good manners that had been so ingrained into her all her life to deal with this unprecedented situation.

'What will you have to drink?' he enquired, gesturing towards the bar.

'Thank you—I'll have a small brandy and water,' she responded—she rarely drank spirits, but she felt she needed something to help her cope with the increasingly bizarre events of the evening.

'Straight Scotch for me, thanks,' put in Adam.

The other man, without being instructed, went round behind the bar to pour their drinks. This one was rather younger than the first—probably only a few years older than Olivia herself. At first sight he could have been taken for a successful accountant or something similar—but no accountant ever wore so many gold rings on his fingers.

He handed her her glass, his eyes wandering over her in an undisguised appraisal, studying every curve, as if he was considering her value on the open market. She returned him a haughty glare down her aristocratic nose. What did he think she was—some piece of fluff that Adam had picked up for one night's entertainment?

The older man laughed. 'That's put you in your place,' he advised him, eyeing Olivia appreciatively. She tried the same look on him, but he wasn't so easily quelled. 'I don't think the young lady is quite sure if she likes us,' he remarked to Adam, faintly amused but not unimpressed.

Adam laughed too, and drew her to his side in a clear statement of possession, letting his hand rest on the slender curve of her hip in a way that made the young accountant's eyes glint with envy. She sipped her brandy, not objecting to the way Adam was holding her; her pulse had quickened with a dangerous excitement at being so close to him.

'I'm afraid I used a certain amount of coercion to bring her here,' he explained easily. 'I don't think she's forgiven me yet.'

'Then perhaps we ought to show her why we invited her?' Harry suggested, moving across the room.

He pulled on a cord that drew back the long red velvet curtain that ran along the length of one wall. Behind it was a window; from waist-height it sloped steeply outwards to look down over the room below. Drawn by a kind of compelling curiosity, she let Adam take her across to look.

She had never really bothered to wonder what the inside of a gambling club would be like. Now she knew. It was a long room, even more dimly lit than the one she was in, though each gaming-table was illuminated by a low light above it, and the air was hazy with cigar-smoke.

There were three roulette wheels down the middle, and at the sides were tables for card-games. The place was crowded—at one of the roulette tables there was laughter, as if people were enjoying themselves, but everywhere else it was clear that gambling was a very serious matter. Even through the glass, she could sense the heat of tension, of large sums of money changing hands.

Nearly all the gamblers were men, their clothes defining their financial status as clearly as the cars parked outside. The few women present seemed to be no more than expensive accessories, the younger and more beautiful the better. The croupiers and the cocktail waitresses too were all very beautiful, their skimpy black satin costumes apparently designed to provide the maximum distraction.

Olivia regarded the scene with distaste. A place like this, pandering to every male vice—what was she supposed to be seeing here that was so important...? And then a man at one of the blackjack tables turned his head slightly, and she caught her breath in shock. Richard!

She stepped back sharply, but Adam caught her, refusing to let her escape. 'It's all right—it's one-way glass. He can't see you,' he told her.

He was holding her there, ruthlessly making her watch as Richard snapped his fingers for one of the waitresses. A leggy blonde, her break-neck curves generously on display, came over to him, flirting with him with her long-lashed eyes. He responded in kind, his eyes lingering over the goods on offer as if he was considering buying. The girl put out a hand, brushing a purely imaginary piece of fluff from his shoulder, and he smiled with intimate interest, patting her pert behind as she moved away to fetch his drink.

A wave of dizziness caught her, and she swayed slightly against Adam. Quickly he steered her to a stool beside the bar and made her sit down. She stared up at him in bewilderment. Had it been some kind of devil's trick she had seen, or had that really been Richard down there?

More brandy appeared in her glass, and she drank it back in a convulsive gulp. The fierce spirit burned her throat, but it seemed to steady her heartbeat. She glared at Adam in cold fury. 'Is this why you brought me here?' she grated between clenched teeth.

He nodded, watching her eyes.

'Why?' she demanded, angry because once again he had manipulated her into being a pawn in his clever game. 'What do you think it's supposed to prove? So he comes to a gambling club occasionally—so do you, apparently.'

'Did you know he would be here?'

'No... but...' She fought desperately to counter the damage he was seeking to do. 'What does it matter? He doesn't have to account to me for his every move.'

'What a very open relationship you have,' he taunted softly.

'If you're going to try to tell me he's cooking the company's books to pay his gambling debts, you can save your breath,' she threw at him, her voice laced with contempt. 'I see everything—all the figures, all the contracts. I'd know if there was anything wrong.'

Adam shook his head. 'I don't know if he's doing anything illegal—not yet. I simply thought you ought to know that your precious Richard isn't quite the virtuous, hard-working, devoted fiancé he pretends to be.'

With a sick realisation she knew that that was true. But she wasn't going to let Adam think he had scored any kind of victory. 'Please take me home,' she requested in glacial accents, rising to her feet.

He smiled drily. 'Very well,' he conceded without argument. 'Goodnight, Harry. And thanks for the information.'

'No trouble,' the older man assured him, shaking his hand in genial farewell. 'The question is, what's your next move?'

'I think I'll wait and see what his will be,' Adam responded grimly.

'He could be unpredictable,' Harry advised. 'I could lend you a couple of my boys to watch your back, if you like.'

Adam grinned, but shook his head. 'Thanks. But I don't think there'll be a problem.'

Harry shrugged. 'As you like. Just let me know if you change your mind.'

Olivia blinked at them in astonishment. What on earth were they talking about? They seemed almost to be implying that *Richard* was the dangerous one. But that was too ridiculous for words. Richard wasn't violent—he was the most gentle man she had ever known.

Of course, it had come as quite a shock to her to see him in a place like this... But then why shouldn't he enjoy a little relaxation if he wanted to? He worked hard enough—too hard, she often thought. She *wouldn't* let Adam sow doubt and confusion in her mind.

But as Harry turned to her, she was startled to see that there was not a trace of cynicism in his level grey eyes. He nodded his head towards Adam. 'You can trust him, you know,' he told her, his voice serious. 'Take it from me—I know an honest man when I meet one.'

She stared at him. He really sounded as if he meant it. But how could he possibly expect her to trust the word of a...a criminal, someone who had been in prison? And yet...there was something strangely compelling in his words, and she felt an odd quaver of uncertainty stir inside her. Was it possible...?

No, they couldn't all have been wrong—the police, the judge, the jury. And besides, she had heard all the evidence herself. There really hadn't been any room for doubt. She would have to be careful—she was in danger of falling into one of Adam's beguiling traps. She must never forget how devious and dangerous he could be.

Ingrained good manners alone dictated her cool, 'Goodnight,' and she turned to precede Adam through the door and down the narrow stairs.

It was a relief to step outside into the cool night air—she felt as if she had escaped from a corner of hell. She disdained Adam's assistance, carefully picking her way by herself across the loose cobbles towards the car. All she wanted to do was get away from here as quickly as possible.

They didn't exchange a single word as they drove home. From time to time Olivia would slant him a covert look from beneath her lashes. His face was as closed and enigmatic as ever. What was he thinking? Did he believe he had scored some kind of victory tonight? He would soon find that he was mistaken—the relationship she shared with Richard was strong enough to withstand his evil machinations.

But still the images she had seen haunted her. That wasn't the Richard she had thought she knew, looking at that girl like that... And he had never once mentioned that place to her, or even hinted that he was aware such establishments existed.

As Adam turned the car into the narrow lane that led down to Beckside she was no closer to reaching any conclusion. He drew the car to a halt on the gravel drive, and switched off the ignition. The silence of the night seemed to wrap around them.

In the darkness she couldn't see his eyes, but she knew that he was watching her. And she was intensely aware of him in the confined space of the car; that subtle male muskiness of his skin haunted her senses, stirring powerful memories that almost seemed to draw her back in time, make her feel once again like a naïve and vulnerable teenager.

'Well? Are you satisfied?' she demanded, retreating from her confusion into a defensive anger. 'I saw what you wanted me to see. But it hasn't

made the slightest difference. Did you really think
that the fact that Richard likes to go out for a little
fun every now and then would be enough to make
me doubt him? Gambling isn't illegal in this
country, you know.'

That cynical smile twisted his hard mouth. 'Such
touching loyalty,' he taunted, a note of dry irony
in his tone. 'You weren't so loyal to me six years
ago, were you?'

He had half turned towards her, resting his elbow
on the back of his seat so that his hand was close
to her face, and almost idly he stroked back a strand
of hair that had escaped from the tight restraint of
its elegant style. She felt a small shiver of heat run
through her, and her mouth was suddenly dry.

'Was it really so very easy for you to believe that
I was a common criminal?' he asked softly. 'It was
purely by good fortune that no night-watchman got
injured in those burglaries—do you think I could
have been a party to something like that?'

'I...' Those dark, hypnotic eyes were weaving
their spell around her, and she was losing her grip
on everything she had thought she was sure of. His
voice was so persuasive, turning everything upside
down...

'Did you really know me so little, trust me so
little?' He was drawing her towards him, his breath
warm against her mouth. 'You told me you loved
me. How could you forget that so easily?'

She couldn't help herself—as his head bent
towards hers, her lips parted in breathless anticipation. His low, husky laughter mocked the ease
of her surrender, but how could she think rationally

when he was close to her like this? She closed her eyes, unable to do anything but let him gather her into his arms and claim her mouth as if it was his by right.

His lips moved over hers, slow and enticing, as his sensuous tongue began an unhurried exploration of all the sweetest, most sensitive membranes within. She was losing her mind, drowning in a whirlpool of sensuous longing that she had neither the will nor the ability to control.

His palm brushed lightly over the firm swell of her breast, stirring the sensitive peak into a ripening response, and she curved herself towards him, shamelessly inviting a repetition of the insolent caress. Even when she felt him slide the tab of her zip down a few inches to loosen her dress so that he could slip it off her shoulder, she couldn't protest.

His touch was warm, smooth, sending a shimmer of exquisite pleasure through her as he stroked her soft skin. The filmy lace cup of her bra was no barrier to him; he simply eased it aside and lifted her naked breast in his long, clever fingers, savouring its ripe fullness. She felt herself melting in response, driven half crazy as with the pad of his thumb he teased the tender bud of her nipple, sending lightning sparks into her brain.

His kiss was becoming deeper, more demanding, his caress ever more possessive. It was like being caught up in some fierce, elemental force that had taken hold of them both. She could sense the barely leashed urgency of a hungry male arousal in him,

but he seemed to be holding it in check—at least
for now.

His control frightened her. He was playing some
game with her, using her body's weakness to break
down her mind's defences, drawing her into his
snares, where he could use her as a weapon against
Richard. She fought to resist him, to retain some
shred of her sanity, but they both knew that he was
winning.

At long last he lifted his head, his eyes dark and
smoky as he gazed down at her. 'You haven't forgotten everything, though, have you, Angel?' he
murmured. 'You haven't forgotten how you used
to want me. Your mind may refuse to admit it, but
your body knows that you belong to me.'

'No——'

'Just take a look at yourself,' he mocked, his
burning gaze flickering down over her. 'Have you
ever been as wanton as this with Richard? I doubt
it. He's got no blood in him—he doesn't know how
to make love to a woman the way you need to be
made love to.'

She tried to shake her head in denial, but her
cheeks flamed scarlet with shame as she realised
that her dress had slipped down over one shoulder,
exposing to his mocking eyes most of the curve of
one creamy breast, tipped with a ripe nub that was
now deep pink in response to his expert caresses,
betraying the truth of what he had said.

He caught her hand away as she tried to make
herself decent, letting his insolent gaze linger over
her nakedness as if he had paid for the privilege.
'If I wanted to take you right here and now in this

car, I could,' he growled, the dark fire in his eyes holding her prisoner. 'You might be wearing his ring on your finger, but it's me you want. Your body's starving for my touch.'

She stared at him, helpless, as with one light fingertip he traced a tantalising path down over the curve of her exposed breast and around the taut aureole, and she couldn't suppress the low moan that broke from her lips. He was enslaving her will, undermining her reason, and she heard herself whisper his name, pleading for more.

'Not here,' he murmured, low and husky, his breath warm against her cheek. 'And not now. But soon. And it will have been worth waiting for— maybe even better now than six years ago. Then you were just a child, innocent and charming but barely half formed. Now you're a woman—all woman. Perfect.'

He bent his head, and placed one single kiss on the tender peak of her nipple, and then abruptly he sat up, and, pulling her dress straight, he fastened the zipper, and then before she could catch her breath he was out of the car and had come round to open her door for her.

Automatically she stepped out of the car, unconscious of the cool night air, her skin still warm from the fires he had generated. 'Don't tell Richard about tonight,' he said, a strange note of seriousness in his voice.

She blinked up at him, memory surging back and with it the guilt and anger. 'Why not?' she countered, haughtily tilting her chin.

His answer was unexpected. 'It could be...dangerous. He has a great deal to lose if he loses you. You give him effective control of the company, and that's all he's ever wanted. It's his obsession, and obsession can make a man irrational.'

She laughed uncertainly. 'You're crazy,' she protested. 'I never heard such utter nonsense in my life!'

'I wish it were nonsense.' Something in his eyes was strangely compelling, and she found herself wavering... He really seemed to believe that what he was saying was true.

Fiercely she shook her head, refusing to let him deceive her. He was the one who was dangerous, not Richard. And he was ruthless—he would try any means at his disposal to achieve his intent. But she wouldn't betray Richard. She owed him that much...

Adam laughed, recognising the battle she was fighting, and knowing just how hard it was. 'I'm not sure what will convince you,' he said. 'But I promise you one thing—I'm not going to let you marry him.'

'You can't stop me,' she insisted tautly.

'We'll see. Oh, by the way...' He took something from his pocket, and handed it to her. 'You'll be wanting these tomorrow when they go to fix your car—it's silly for you to get new ones when these are perfectly OK.'

'What are they?' she asked blankly.

'The fuses.' His eyes glinted with pure devilish amusement as he winked at her, and then he strolled back round the car and slid in behind the wheel. The engine purred to life like a big cat, and the gravel crunched as he pulled away. She stood and watched as the red tail-lights disappeared into the darkness.

Slowly her racing heartbeat began to steady. But she knew it would be a complete waste of time going to bed—she was far too wound-up to sleep. Instead she turned her footsteps down through the quiet garden, and found herself presently at the door of the summer-house. Pushing it open, she went inside.

It was strange, she reflected, that she should have sought out this place, almost unconsciously. It had been here that she had always come as a retreat when she was small, and Eleanor's nagging had got too much for her. And here was where she and Adam had come to be alone, during those few blissful weeks when they had been together. And here too was where she had come when she had needed to be alone, after he was arrested. But until the day of Lex's funeral he hadn't been down here for several years.

Why had Adam had to come back? Her life had been well-ordered and calm—all he had done was stir up the pain of old memories, reawaken old doubts and confusions. He was so clever, weaving his deceiving spells, until she didn't know which was truth and which was lies.

But how *could* she have any doubts? Had time faded her recall of the details, making her forget why, at the time, she had been so sure? Surely she could never forget that day, the day when her whole world had fallen apart.

She had been in seventh heaven, so in love, so excited at the thought of her wedding. Every little detail was going to be perfect—nothing could possibly go wrong. And her dress—it was like something out of a fairy-tale...

CHAPTER SEVEN

ALL frills and lace and white satin bows. She had spent ages standing patiently before the mirror at the dressmakers, having dozens of tiny adjustments made, dreamily imagining Adam's face as he saw her floating down the aisle towards him.

The fitting was almost over when the telephone rang. Mrs James went to answer it, and then called her over. 'It's your stepmother,' she told her.

Olivia blinked in surprise—what on earth could Eleanor want? So far she had taken very little interest in the wedding—she thought it was all far too rushed, and that she was far too young. She took the receiver with a curious, 'Hello?'

Eleanor's voice was brusque. 'I'm at the hospital,' she announced without preamble. 'You'd better come over right away. It's Lex... he's had a stroke.'

'What?' Her head seemed to spin. 'But... Is he all right?'

'He's in Intensive Care.'

'Oh...' Guiltily Olivia realised that her first thought had been not for her father's health, but for the possible delay to her own wedding plans. Quickly she put such selfishness aside. 'I'll come straight away,' she promised. 'It won't take me long.'

The dressmaker took the receiver from her numb fingers, and set it back on its rest. 'Whatever's the matter?' she enquired solicitously. 'You've gone as white as a sheet.'

'My father—he's been rushed to hospital,' she explained, a new wave of shock riding over her. *Lex*, seriously ill? But he was *never* ill. He wasn't like ordinary mortals, prone to the occasional weakness—he'd never even had a cold!

'Dear, dear! Has there been an accident?'

'No—he's...had a stroke. I have to go over there right away.' Distractedly she began trying to reach for the zip that fastened the tight basque-top of her dress.

'Here—let me help you with that,' Mrs James offered quickly. 'Are you quite sure you feel able to drive yourself? I could call a taxi for you.'

'No—it's all right, I'll be all right.' It wasn't far to the hospital, and Adam would be there to drive her home afterwards. She changed quickly out of her wedding-dress into the cotton summer dress she had been wearing. By then she had recovered enough composure to thank Mrs James for her kindness.

'I hope you find him well,' the dressmaker called as she waved her goodbye. 'Don't worry about your dress—just call me, and we can finish off any time you want.'

The short drive to the hospital was like a waking nightmare. What if Lex should die? If only Adam had been able to come and fetch her—and why hadn't *he* rung her, instead of Eleanor? But perhaps he hadn't wanted to leave Lex's side. It would be all right with Adam there—somehow she felt that he would be able to give some of his strength to Lex, just by holding his hand.

It came as rather a surprise to find that it was Richard who met her at the entrance to the hospital. 'Where's Adam?' she asked first.

Why did he seem to hesitate? Did he disapprove that her initial thoughts didn't seem to be for Lex? 'I'll explain in a minute,' he said. 'Come on—it's this way.' He took her arm. 'I'm afraid you're going to have to prepare yourself—he looks very ill indeed.'

'Is he going to die?' she whispered.

He shook his head. 'I don't think so. But he's on a ventilator, and the doctors say there's no way of knowing at present how much damage has been caused. It was a very serious stroke.'

She shook her head, bewildered. 'I don't understand—he seemed so well this morning. How could it just come out of the blue like that?' She glanced up at him, and saw how grim his expression was. 'What happened?' she asked, a cold chill, a premonition of disaster, creeping into her heart. 'What caused it?'

Suddenly a strange quiet seemed to have settled around them; all the little noises of the hospital—the echo of voices, the clank of metal trolleys—had faded away. Richard hesitated again, and then drew her over to sit down in a quiet alcove away from the busy corridor. He held both her hands in his, and looked straight into her eyes. 'Adam's been arrested,' he told her gently.

'*What?*' Again her head seemed to spin, this time much more alarmingly.

'It's to do with that Chinese vase that was found by Customs in one of our crates. The police have been around for a couple of days, asking questions——'

'Yes, I know that.'

'Well, they seem to think they've found some evidence to tie Adam in with the theft,' he explained, his voice conveying his own disbelief. 'They came and arrested him this morning. Lex was furious—I've never seen him so worked up. I tried to persuade him to calm down, but he was shouting and making threats—and then quite suddenly he just collapsed. I thought at first it was a heart attack, but the doctors say it's a stroke.'

'But... I don't understand,' she whispered, totally bewildered. 'How could the police possibly think Adam would have had anything to do with stealing a vase?'

He shook his head, his own expression puzzled. 'I don't know—I can't make sense of it either. I mean, *Adam,* of all people! After all, it's not as if he would need the money or anything. It just seems completely incredible to me.'

She was shaking uncontrollably. 'It can't be true—there must be some mistake...'

He put his arm around her, and drew her head down on to his shoulder, soothing her as she began to cry. 'I'm sure there is. Don't worry, there must be some explanation. Once we know a little more about it all...'

Great painful sobs were racking her body and soaking the lapels of Richard's smart grey business suit. Without a word he gave her a handkerchief, and she soaked that instead, as he patiently comforted her, until at last the tears subsided enough for her to lift her head.

'I'm sorry,' she mumbled, realising the damage she had done to his suit.

'That's all right.' He smiled down at her. 'Do you feel up to visiting Lex yet?'

She nodded. 'In a minute.' Resolutely she struggled to pull herself together, blowing her nose and reaching into her handbag for her make-up mirror. She looked awful, her eyes swollen and red, her nose shiny. She didn't have much make-up—she rarely wore it—but she did what she could to disguise the ravages of her tears, and then looked up at Richard, managing a watery smile. 'OK,' she said.

He kept his arm reassuringly round her shoulders as he led her down the corridor, and in through a set of swing doors. The sight that met her eyes chilled her to the bone, and she was glad of Richard's strength to support her. It was like something out of a science-fiction nightmare.

There was so much equipment—green dials flashing, things bleeping, clear liquid in plastic sacs swung from chrome stands... And in the middle of it all, lying flat on a kind of trolley instead of a bed, was Lex, his face as pale and mottled and cold as marble.

Eleanor was sitting stiffly in a straight-backed chair, as if she didn't quite know how she was supposed to behave in this alien environment. As Olivia and Richard entered, she rose to her feet.

'How is he?' Richard asked, his voice only a little above a whisper.

'Oh...' Eleanor made a vague gesture with her hand. 'Much the same, I think.'

Olivia moved slowly towards the trolley; why was everyone talking as if they were in church? Her father looked...smaller, somehow, as if some of his fierce spirit had already left his body. There was a plastic mouthpiece between his lips, keeping his airway open, and the nurse standing behind his head smiled at her.

'He's breathing on his own now.'

'Oh...' That sounded promising, at least. 'Is he going to be all right?'

'It's a bit too early to say. But a lot of people recover completely after a stroke, or are maybe left with just a little bit of disability.'

Olivia nodded. She was sure the nurse meant to be reassuring, but at the moment she couldn't imagine Lex ever getting up from this trolley again. And she certainly couldn't imagine him disabled— not Lex. And this had happened because of Adam...?

A shiver ran through her. Why had the police arrested him? They must have been very sure of their evidence... Nervously she twisted the sapphire and diamond ring on her finger—the ring he had put there just two weeks ago. She had thought at the time, with a kind of fatalistic apprehension, that such incredible happiness was too unreal to last...

Richard touched her arm. 'Do you want to stay for a little while?' he asked. 'Only I'm going to run Eleanor home now.'

'Oh... Yes, I'll stay. Thank you...' Her voice choked, and she sat down in the seat that Eleanor had left. It wasn't so much that she wanted to be with Lex—he had no idea that she was here, and anyway they had never had a great deal to say to each other. She just needed to be alone, to try and make sense of what had happened. She had barely had a chance to come to terms with having all her dreams come true when they had been cruelly snatched away from her again.

When Richard returned, several hours later, it was to find her sitting in the same position, like a zombie. When he asked if she was ready to leave she just nodded, and he took her hand and led her out of the hospital and across the car park to his car.

'I've heard from Adam's solicitor,' he told her gently as he climbed in beside her.

She looked up at him with wide, hopeful eyes.

'He's been charged. They're hoping to get him bail in the morning, but the prosecution are likely to contest it, at least at this stage.'

'Where is he?' she whispered. 'Will they let me see him?'

He shook his head. 'Not at the moment. Maybe in a day or two——'

'Do *you* think he did it?' she asked—suddenly it was very important to her to have an independent viewpoint. She looked searchingly into Richard's eyes, determined not to let him deceive her.

'I ... don't know.' But he was holding back; he suspected that it was true. To evade her probing he started the car, and pulled slowly forward to the road. 'We'll find out more in a day or two. They'll have to produce enough evidence to convince a magistrate.'

'Yes.' At least she could pin her hopes on that. If it was all a mistake—if it *was* all a mistake—the Magistrates' Court would set him free.

But it didn't. She had wanted to go to the hearing, but she wasn't able to bring herself to face it—she was afraid that she wouldn't be able to hold back the tears. But Richard had attended, and when he returned, his face was grave.

'They've remanded him in custody for a further seven days,' he told her.

Olivia felt her heart sinking. 'Was it bad?'

'It doesn't look too good,' he conceded. 'Apparently his car was identified at the scene.'

'But it's quite a common car,' she protested, clutching at straws. 'It could have been another one that looked the same.'

'The tyre prints matched.'

He wrote to her from prison. She felt slightly sick as she opened the envelope, to find the white fold of lined prison notepaper inside. What had she been hoping for? Some kind of explanation? An apology? But there was none—just a persuasive assurance that he was innocent, and a plea to her to come and visit him.

For a little while she wavered. Maybe it *had* all been some ghastly mistake, after all—though she couldn't see how. Even Richard couldn't think of a plausible explanation that would account for his car's having been at the scene of the crime.

'Maybe the real thieves stole it, and returned it without him realising it?' he suggested as for the umpteenth time they turned to discussing the subject over the dinner table.

'Back into his locked garage?' queried Eleanor drily. 'I hardly think that's very likely.'

'But what if someone was deliberately trying to frame him?'

'And who would want to do that?' Eleanor had never made any secret of the fact that she had believed Adam guilty from the start. 'I dare say he's got as many enemies as anyone else, but I certainly can't think of anyone who would want to go to such lengths. Can you?'

'Well . . .'

'Precisely,' concluded Eleanor in triumph. 'I'm afraid that so far as I'm concerned it really doesn't come as that much of a surprise. I never trusted him. Oh, he was very charming, I grant you—but then his type usually are. Lex could never see it, of course—anyone would have thought he was his own son! I suppose having him for a son-in-law was second best—he was so delighted by the idea, he couldn't see what he was up to.'

Olivia stared at her. 'Wh . . . what do you mean?' she questioned, puzzled.

Eleanor turned to her, her own kind of brusque sympathy in her voice. 'I'm sorry dear, but I don't believe in mincing words. You're very young, and you couldn't be expected to know how a man like that operates. The fact is, he couldn't be content with just one third of the shares in the company—he could never be completely sure of retaining control. He needed your third as well.'

'Oh...' As the appalling realisation of the truth of what Eleanor had said sunk in, Olivia excused herself swiftly from the table, and fled. Of course—what a fool she had been! How could she ever have been so vain and stupid as to think she could win Adam's love so easily, when all the other girls who had set their caps at him had failed? She had had a unique attraction, all right—but it wasn't the kind she had so naïvely imagined.

Richard had come after her, catching her as she reached the haven of the summer-house and taking her into his arms as she collapsed in tears. 'Don't cry,' he whispered, stroking her hair with a soothing hand. 'I'm sure Eleanor's wrong—I'm sure that isn't why he wanted to marry you.'

'No.' She shook her head fiercely. 'She's right. Oh, what an idiot I've been. I thought he loved me...'

'Now, now. Don't cry—you'll make yourself ill. And you don't want to do that at the moment, do you? You want to be able to visit Lex.'

The mention of her father, so ill in hospital, brought a stab of guilt. But it steeled her backbone, and she stood up straight, fighting back her tears. 'Of course,' she agreed bravely. A new hardness had crept into her heart. It was because of Adam that Lex had had his stroke—even more than what he had done to her, she would never forgive him for that. 'And I'm sure Eleanor's right about him committing those burglaries, as well,' she asserted. 'I mean, for one thing, it seems strange that no one saw him that night, after he left the squash club.'

'But that doesn't prove anything,' Richard argued seriously.

'It doesn't disprove anything, either.'

When a second letter arrived, addressed in Adam's handwriting, she threw it away unopened.

Fortunately Lex's stout constitution enabled him to survive the stroke. Within a few days he was moved out of Intensive Care and into a pleasant private room on the first floor. But as the weeks passed his recovery was slow; he couldn't speak properly, his face looked odd, pulled down on one side, and he couldn't use his right hand.

Olivia had just returned from visiting him when, letting herself into the house, she had heard the telephone ringing. She ran to pick it up, fearing bad news from the hospital. But it was Adam's voice she heard.

'Hello, Angel. How are you?'

A chill of ice ran through her. 'Good afternoon, Adam,' she managed, her voice stiff.

'How's Lex?' he asked—how easy it was for him to sound concerned, when she couldn't see his face, she reflected acidly.

'He's recovering, thank you,' she responded with dignity.

She sensed that he was taken aback by the coldness of her tone. 'Did you get my letters?' he asked.

'Yes.'

'Did you read them?'

'I read the first one,' she responded tautly, afraid of the beguiling spells his voice could weave even when he wasn't there in the flesh.

'Angel, you don't really think I did it, do you?'

'I . . . I'd really rather not speak to you, Adam,' she insisted, her heart twisting with pain.

'Angel, please listen to me——'

She put the phone down quickly. That voice was so persuasive . . . She knew that if she gave him the least chance he could convince her that the world was flat and the moon was made of cream cheese. After all, he had managed to convince her that he loved her.

After that one call, he made no further attempt to contact her—she wasn't sure if that was a relief or a disappointment. But slowly her heart began to heal, and by the time his trial came up in the Crown Court, four months later, she felt strong enough to face it. Somehow she felt it was important for her to attend, to listen to every word that was said, to banish once and for all any last vestige of doubt that might be lingering in her mind.

It was three weeks after Christmas, a cold, dismal January. She sat in the back row of the public gallery with Richard as the evidence was spelled out with neat legalistic precision. And when it came to the turn of the defence to try to refute it, the result seemed to be beyond reasonable doubt.

The jury evidently felt the same—their verdict was unanimous. Guilty. Adam stood, handcuffed to a police warden, to hear the judge's closing words—he didn't even have the grace to bow his head. Maybe that arrogance even caused the judge to add a few more months to his sentence.

Three years.

A murmur rippled round the courtroom as it was announced. 'He's got off fairly lightly,' Richard commented quietly. 'First offence. With full remission, and parole, he'll probably be out in a year.'

A year. It was almost impossible to comprehend—to be shut away in a prison cell for a whole year...

And then as they led him away to the cells he turned, and looked up—straight at the back row of the public gallery, as if he had known that she had been there all the time. Her heart seemed to stop beating as he stared at her for what felt like a few seconds of eternity. If the eyes were the windows on the soul, then he had no soul...

There were tears on her cheeks as she drew herself back out of those painful memories. It had hurt to remember it all in so much detail—but it had been important that she should remind herself of just how treacherous Adam could be.

How could she love a man like that? And yet... she did. There—she had finally admitted it. It had been gnawing at her heart ever since the day he had come back—indeed it had been there for the past six years, dormant but never completely extinguished.

So, having acknowledged that unwelcome fact, what of the future? She certainly had no intention of letting Adam lure her any deeper into his coils. He would be quite unscrupulous about using her—she knew that already. And she would not be the instrument of his revenge on Richard.

Richard... Her thoughts went back to that unsavoury scene she had witnessed earlier in the night. She would never have dreamed that he was secretly visiting a place like that. Was there anything else that she didn't know about him...?

Briskly she shook her head. It had been precisely Adam's intention to sow these seeds of doubt—and she wasn't going to let him succeed. Quite how she could raise the subject with Richard she wasn't sure—she would have to tell him that she had been spying on him, however unwillingly. But discuss it with him she would—that was the only way to draw the sting of Adam's evil schemes.

If only there were a little more time... The wedding was only one week away; everything had been arranged, down to the printing of the programmes for the order of the service, the flower-arrangements to decorate the tables at the reception.

Again she was aware of the feeling of being on a moving escalator, carried along by forces outside her own control; the days were passing, and she could do nothing to hold them back. But to cancel everything now—even simply to postpone it—would be terribly hurtful to Richard, and would, in a sense, give Adam his victory.

But was it right to marry Richard, knowing how she felt about Adam? She *could* be happy with him—he was kind and understanding, and had never demanded too much of her. But could he be happy with her? He knew that she had loved Adam before—maybe he had even guessed the way things still were. It must be terribly hard for him.

But he would be patient, and she *would* make him happy. And in time, maybe she would be able to put her memories of Adam back into that remote corner of her mind where they would have the least effect on her day-to-day life.

Somewhere in the distance an owl hooted, and a fox's cry pierced the night. With a small jolt of surprise she realised that it was very late, and the cold night air was penetrating her thin silky dress and jacket. She could deal with no more problems tonight. Wearily she rose to her feet, rubbing her hands over her arms to warm them a little, and set off back to the house.

Rather to her surprise, she slept well, better than she had for several weeks—it must have been sheer emotional exhaustion. She woke to a beautiful September morning, and decided to take Kelly, her young bay mare, for a long gallop over the hills above Beckside.

The trees were just beginning to turn to their autumn colours, and there was a fresh breeze in the air to blow away the cobwebs. But she couldn't completely relax and enjoy her ride—all the time she was on edge, listening for the sound of other hoofs, watching for any glimpse of a large black hunter in pursuit.

There was no sign of Adam—but as she cantered gently back to the stables she saw Richard's car turn into the drive. By the time she had unsaddled Kelly, and handed her over to the groom, he was walking down to meet her. Still uncertain about what she was going to say to him, she moved towards him.

'Hello.' Her voice sounded strange even to her own ears. 'I wasn't expecting to see you this weekend.'

He smiled—that open, honest smile that gave him such a boyish look. 'I'm playing truant,' he admitted frankly, falling into step beside her. 'I thought perhaps we might drive out and have lunch somewhere.'

'That would be very nice,' she managed. 'I suppose...' The sun was still shining, but a dark shadow seemed to be surrounding just the two of them—a dark shadow of suspicion. 'I suppose you were working very late last night?' she queried, almost hating herself for not having the courage to ask him an honest question.

'Actually I chucked it in about ten,' he confessed. 'I thought about coming on to Felicity's, but it seemed rather too late—and besides, I doubt if I'd have been very good company,' he added a little sheepishly. 'I needed to unwind.'

She slanted him a look of enquiry, her heart tense.

That smile took on a wry twist. 'As a matter of fact, I went to a little club I know in Nottingham—not the sort of place I could ever take you, I'm afraid.'

A great wave of relief flooded through her. Of course she should never have doubted him. How could there be anything sinister about it, when he had brought it all out into the open so readily? She slanted him a teasing look. 'Why couldn't you take me?' she enquired lightly. 'Wouldn't I approve?'

He laughed, slipping a casual arm around her shoulders. 'No, I'm afraid you wouldn't,' he responded, though his eyes were smiling. 'It involves a little bit of a flutter on the cards, and some rather scantily clad ladies.'

'Really?' She was enjoying playing the unshockable sophisticate. 'It sounds interesting.'

He chuckled with laughter. 'Maybe I will take you there one day, at that,' he mused. 'Anyway, how are all the arrangements for the wedding? Have you and Eleanor spent a fortune? I'm afraid I haven't really had time to be as involved as I would have liked to be.'

Olivia hesitated—the dilemma of last night still troubling her mind. She lowered her eyes, afraid that he would see too much in them.

'Olivia?' She couldn't miss the catch in his voice. 'Is there . . . something wrong?'

How on earth could she explain? She wasn't even sure herself which course she ought to take.

'Olivia . . .' His hand was shaking as he reached for her. Passively she let him draw her into his arms. 'It's Adam, isn't it?' The pain in his voice twisted the knife of guilt in her heart. 'I was afraid of this, from the moment he showed up. You . . . still love him, don't you?'

'I . . . don't know,' she whispered, unable to bring herself to admit it fully to him.

His arms tightened around her in a possessive grip. 'You know I love you, my darling,' he murmured, awkward with expressing such deep emotion. 'But if I thought . . . if I thought he could make you happy, I'd stand aside. I love you that much. But I know he doesn't really care for you.'

'I know that too,' she managed, forcing herself to look up at him. 'That's why . . . that's why . . .'

'You're not having second thoughts about marrying me, are you?' he pleaded, a look almost of desperation in his eyes. '*Please*, Olivia. It doesn't matter if you don't love me—I love you enough for both of us.'

'But I *do* love you,' she protested, reaching out for that amid all the confusion.

His whole face lit with happiness. 'Then you don't want to cancel the wedding?' he questioned anxiously.

'No, I don't want to cancel the wedding.' What else could she say?

'Oh, my darling.' He drew her close against him, burying his face in her hair, and she could feel his body trembling. 'I was so afraid you were going to change your mind. I'll do everything I can to make you happy, darling, I promise. You're my whole world.'

She rested her cheek against his shoulder, feeling a sense of peace inside her now that she had made her final decision. She couldn't have brought herself to have broken his heart, not after all these years—he didn't deserve that. She would do all she could to make him happy, too, to make their marriage work. Adam had almost wrecked her life once—she wouldn't allow him the opportunity to do it again.

'There's just one thing,' Richard added, a tentative note in his voice.

She looked up at him, puzzled.

He smiled wryly. 'Maybe I'm being a little over-anxious, but I can't help fearing that he'll stop at nothing to prevent our wedding.' His blue eyes were serious. 'I'm so afraid he might try to hurt you. I'd like you to have a bodyguard.'

Her eyes registered her amazement. 'A *body-guard*?' What a strange irony, that only last night Adam had been accusing Richard of planning her harm. It was crazy, the depth of hatred and suspicion between the two men. And once they had been friends...

'Just until the wedding,' Richard pleaded, deeply earnest. 'Once we're safely married, I'm hoping he'll give up wasting his time, and leave us alone. But until then... It would stop me worrying about you.'

She hesitated. She knew it was completely unnecessary, but... well, if it made him feel better. 'All right,' she agreed, smiling up at him in fond humour. 'It'll make me feel like Madonna or something. But if you think I should have one,' she added, frowning, 'what about you? I would have thought he's far more likely to try and hurt you than me.'

He laughed, shaking his head. 'Oh, you don't need to worry about me,' he assured her with calm confidence. 'I can take care of myself.'

CHAPTER EIGHT

WELL, this was it—the big day. Everyone else had already left for the church—the bridesmaids, squabbling and sulky, towing the reluctant pageboy, who would have much preferred to be out scrumping apples than posing about in an itchy velvet suit. Eleanor, in a very chic creation in sugar-pink with a cartwheel hat to match, that she had decided just twenty minutes before she had been due to leave wasn't really quite what she had wanted after all. And Georgina, unconventional but not too outrageous in a purple satin suit, slanting Olivia secret smug glances that made her wonder what Adam had been doing this past week.

Adam ... It troubled her that she couldn't stop thinking about him. But at least one advantage of having a burly bodyguard always around had been that he hadn't even attempted to pester her any more. She hadn't even seen him—at least, not so that she could be sure. She had had the feeling, while they were running through the wedding re-hearsal in the church on Wednesday evening, that someone was watching them from the shadows up in the gallery, but when she had looked she hadn't been able to see anyone.

And now the car was outside, and her uncle Gerald—Lex's only brother—was waiting down-stairs in his smart morning-suit to escort her to the church in Lex's place. Out in the garden, a huge red and white marquee covered tables laden with a ton of food, an exquisitely iced wedding cake of four tiers, and enough champagne to float a battleship.

She stood in front of the cheval mirror in her bedroom, taking a last long look at her own reflection. The next time she looked at herself in a mirror, she would be Mrs Richard Simpson. Firmly she repressed the uncomfortable little niggle of doubt that still kept intruding itself into her mind. She *was* doing the right thing . . . wasn't she?

So why was she constantly comparing this with that other wedding she had dreamed of and planned all those years ago? Suddenly she found herself wondering what had happened to that beautiful dress that Mrs James had been making for her—odd that it had never occurred to her to wonder about that before. Had it been cut up, and used in other people's wedding dresses afterwards? It seemed so sad that it should have come to such an anonymous end—it had been *such* a beautiful dress.

This one was similar, but . . . it could never be quite the same. It was of a rustling silk taffeta, with a low sweetheart neckline trimmed with taffeta roses, and a full, heavy skirt that swept the ground in a short train behind her. Her long white veil was held in place by the same kind of taffeta roses, and her bouquet was of white and pink roses, in clouds of white gypsophila. A perfect picture—so long as no one looked too closely into her eyes.

And suddenly as she stood gazing at herself, it was as if she was seeing a stranger. A freezing chill seemed to be creeping into her heart. She shouldn't be doing this—it wasn't fair to Richard to be marrying him, when she was in love with Adam. She couldn't go through with it . . .

'Olivia? Is everything all right?' Uncle Gerald's call from downstairs cut sharply across her thoughts. 'We ought to be going, you know— Richard will be getting worried.'

With a sinking feeling, she realised that she had left it too late—she had to go through with it now. She couldn't just leave Richard standing at the altar, in front of all those people—she couldn't be that cruel. Sternly she faced herself. She had promised herself that she would make him happy, and she must live the rest of her life by that promise. And maybe in time the emptiness in her own heart would be filled by his gentle affection.

'I'm . . . coming,' she called, and with her bouquet in one hand she lifted the heavy train of her skirt, and hurried down the stairs.

Uncle Gerald watched her descent, his ruddy face beaming. 'You look lovely,' he declared warmly. 'Lex would have been so proud of you.'

Yes, she reminded herself tartly—and if it hadn't been for Adam Lex wouldn't have had his stroke, and he might have been here today, to lead her down the aisle, as he ought to be. The recollection of that fact would give her the courage not to waver at the very last moment. Impulsively she leaned up and kissed her old uncle on the cheek. 'Thank you,' she whispered.

He coloured with pleasure. 'Well, come on, we'd best be getting off,' he bustled, stubbing his thick

cigar in a Wedgwood dish on the sideboard—
Eleanor would have a fit when she discovered the
pungent residue, Olivia reflected with wry humour.
Then she slipped her hand through his arm, and let
him lead her out of the front door.

A white Rolls-Royce, tricked out with yards of
white satin ribbons, stood in the drive, the back
door ajar. Uncle Gerald handed her into it, and she
settled herself carefully on the cream leather up-
holstery as he folded the voluminous folds of her
skirt carefully around her ankles so that it wouldn't
crease too much.

'There—mind your veil,' he warned.

She drew the drift of net back out of the way,
smiling her thanks to him as he closed the door and
began to walk ponderously round the back of the
car to the other side. Closing her eyes, she tried
hard to concentrate her mind. She was going to
marry Richard. Just a few more minutes, and
then——

She opened her eyes sharply as the car jerked
away with a crunch of gravel, leaving Uncle Gerald
standing on the drive staring after it in open-
mouthed astonishment. 'What the...?' And then
she saw the chauffeur's eyes in the rear-view
mirror—dark, dangerous eyes, that were smiling
back at her in amused satisfaction.

'Hello, Angel.'

'What the hell do you think you're doing?' she
exploded in hot fury. 'Stop this car at once!'

'Sorry about the melodrama, Angel,' he drawled
laconically. 'But I did warn you that I wasn't going
to let you marry Richard.'

'You're crazy! Let me out this minute.' As the car slowed its pace a little for the turn from the end of the drive into the road lane she grabbed at the door-handle, but it wouldn't open.

'No, don't try to throw yourself out,' he advised, smiling with a hint of lazy mockery. 'The doors are locked.'

She sat back in the corner of the seat, struggling to control the urge to panic. Had Adam gone completely mad? Richard had warned her that he might try to harm her, and she hadn't believed him. Now it seemed he had been right all along. She had to try and remain cool if she possibly could. She had been kidnapped by a madman, a man obsessed by some kind of twisted desire for revenge. He might even be planning to kill her.

He had taken off his chauffeur's cap—how effective that had been as a disguise, when he had been the last person she had been expecting to see at the wheel of the car anyway. Now she came to think of it, she had thought it slightly odd that he had stayed in the car when they had come out of the house, instead of holding the door open, but she had had other things on her mind at the time.

'Well—you've been very clever,' she conceded acidly. 'How did you get your hands on the car? Did you bribe the real chauffeur—or knock him out?'

He laughed. 'Oh, nothing so drastic. I simply rang the firm this morning and told them there had been a slight change to the arrangements, and they were to pick you up twenty minutes later.'

As he spoke, another white Rolls-Royce passed them, ribbons waving in the breeze, heading back in the direction from which they had just come. Too late Olivia thought of trying to attract the driver's attention—the car had already passed them. Grating her teeth in frustration, she sat back again.

'I'm sorry I had to do it this way, Angel,' he remarked, still with that infuriating smile of satisfaction on his face. 'It's been quite a problem—with that squad of minders he's had surrounding you this past week I haven't been able to get near you.'

She returned him only a cold stare.

He laughed softly. 'Poor old Ricky, standing there at the altar waiting for his beautiful bride, only to find he's been jilted at the very last minute.'

'I hate you.' Her voice held all the more venom because she had come so close to jilting Richard herself, not ten minutes ago. 'You'll get caught, and you'll go to prison for a very long time. And I won't care!' she added fiercely, though she knew that she would, and that he knew it too.

He shook his head, his eyes glinting with dark wickedness. 'Oh, I've no intention of going to prison,' he responded softly. 'I think maybe by the time the police catch up with us you'll be more than willing to tell them it was all a misunderstanding.'

Her cheeks flamed a heated scarlet, and she snatched her gaze away from his. 'Never!' she asserted, turning to glare angrily out of the side-window.

He had turned off the main road into the quiet country lanes, and there were no other cars around, no one who could rescue her or raise the alarm. Where on earth was he taking her? She looked around, trying to catch a glimpse of some kind of reference point, but the high hedges that lined the road hid everything from sight.

It was a surprise when he turned the car off the road into a small copse of trees. A large closed horse-box was waiting there, and as she watched in bewildered amazement he climbed out of the Rolls-Royce and went over to it, opening the back doors. There was no horse, and no hay, inside—just two planks of wood which he let down to the ground. Then he came back to the car, and with infinite care drove it up the planks and into the horse-box.

'There.' He turned to her, smiling that devil's smile. 'Don't worry—it's not too far to go now.'

She refused even to look at him, and with a dry laugh he eased himself out of the restricted gap of the door of the Rolls-Royce, and walked to the back of the horse-box. She heard him jump down, heard him slide the planks back into place, and then the doors closed, leaving her in almost total darkness. A few moments later the engine of the horse-box started up, and it drove away.

She was his prisoner. No one seeing an innocent horse-box trundling around the country roads would suspect that there was a white Rolls-Royce inside, and a kidnap victim in a stupid wedding dress. Impatiently she snatched off her veil, and tossed it down on the seat beside her.

Oh, his planning had been absolutely brilliant, she was forced to concede. And he had carried it out so smoothly—but of course he had had plenty of experience in criminal enterprises. And to think she had almost begun to believe that it had all been some kind of terrible mistake, that he had been innocent!

Where were they going? Consciously she tried to focus on the route they were taking, to remember each turning—maybe then if she got a chance to escape she would be able to find her way quickly back. But with no point of visual reference it was impossible to maintain a sense of direction.

Poor Richard—what must he be going through now? Uncle Gerald would have rung the church straight away—it must have been a terrible shock for him. And already the police would have been alerted—there would be road-blocks, helicopters, every vehicle in the area would be stopped and searched.

What would Adam do if they stopped him? He had been very clever so far—could he bluff his way through? Surely not—they would know that he was the one who had kidnapped her, and his picture would have been circulated, they would recognise him at once.

And he would go back to prison. Her heart contracted in sudden pain—the thought of him being locked up again, in such indignity… She ought not to be thinking like that, but somehow she just couldn't bring herself to be as angry with him, as afraid of him, as she knew she ought to be. And somehow she knew that he wouldn't really hurt her.

Much sooner than she had expected, it seemed that they had reached their destination. The horse-box drew to a halt, and she heard Adam climb out of the cab, leaving the engine running. A moment later he was back, and the changing sounds told her that he had driven into a garage.

She tensed as the back doors of the horse-box opened—this might be her last chance to escape. But as he came to open the door of the Rolls-Royce, she realised that the garage doors were closed. She might have known that he wouldn't overlook a simple thing like that.

It was quite a large garage, with space for at least four cars, though only his grey Aston Martin was there. A bare lightbulb hung from the ceiling, and against the back wall was a workbench. A flight of open wooden stairs rose to the floor above, where she guessed there were quarters for a chauffeur. The place was probably attached to some large house—but which?

'Come on,' he ordered, reaching into the car to take her wrist.

'All right,' she snapped, shaking herself free. 'I'm coming. There's no need to get rough.'

He chuckled with laughter. 'Very well, your ladyship,' he taunted. 'If you would care to step this way?'

He stood back, and allowed her to climb from the back of the car herself. It was a slight squeeze, because the door wouldn't open fully in the confined space of the horse-box. And then she had to jump to the ground, as he stood watching her, a mocking smile on his face.

As she scrambled down, she heard the ominous rip, and looked round. Her skirt had snagged on something, and a great jagged tear had sliced into the silk. She stared at it in horror. It could never be mended—the dress was ruined... As if that mattered, she scolded herself, feeling almost on the verge of hysteria. She had been kidnapped—she wasn't going to be appearing at her wedding. She didn't even know if she would ever be seen alive again!

Impatiently she dragged the skirt free, making the tear even worse, and as Adam stood aside, gesturing with feigned gallantry for her to precede him, she stalked up the stairs, her head held at a haughty angle.

She found herself in a large room, comfortably if cheaply furnished. In one corner was a kind of kitchenette, equipped with a sink and a small cooker. There was a television, and a couple of armchairs. And there was a large pine-framed double bed, covered with a brightly coloured patchwork quilt.

She stood and stared at the bed, a thud of panic making her heart beat faster. Adam came up behind her. 'I'm sorry, Angel,' he said seriously. 'I'm going to have to tie you up now. I'm going to leave you for a while, and I can't have you trying to escape.'

She stared up at him, a chill of fear shivering through her. Suddenly she was aware of just how dangerous he was. Perhaps, for the moment at least, it would be better to do as he said. There was no telling what he might do if she attempted to disobey him. Reluctantly she allowed him to draw her hands together behind her back, standing passive, offering him no resistance.

He tied her wrists firmly with a silk scarf, and then her ankles, and then tied another round her mouth in a gag, carefully checking that there was no way she would be able to scream or call for help. And then he scooped her up in his arms, and carried her over to lay her down on the bed.

Her eyes gazed up into his. What was he planning to do with her, now that he had brought her here? Whatever his intentions, she would be quite unable to defend herself, with her hands tied behind her back. Lying there, her body seemed to be curved towards him invitingly, and she couldn't help but be acutely aware of the way her ragged breathing crushed her tender breasts against the whale-boned bodice of her dress—and as his dark gaze was drawn there, almost as if against his will, she felt a shimmer of heat run through her. If he was planning to rape her...

A breath of a sigh escaped him. 'Oh, Angel...' He sat down on the bed beside her, and his hand stroked gently over her cheek. 'Don't cry, Angel, and don't be afraid,' he murmured, his voice as soft and tender as a kiss. 'You know I would never hurt you. I had to do this.'

Those eyes... She could drown in their depths, lose herself forever. She had forgotten that he had kidnapped her on the way to her own wedding. He was her lover; he had carried her away to some secret hiding-place, where they would make love for ever and ever...

Something inside her seemed to crack at that moment. She had loved him for so long, and she had fought to resist it. But now she could fight it no more. She was helpless, his prisoner, not knowing what fate he had in store for her. And she loved him. If only he had hijacked her because he loved her too, and not just to serve his revenge on Richard... If only he loved her, then she would go to the ends of the earth for him. No matter what he was, no matter what he had done, she would stand by him.

As if he could read her thoughts, he smiled slowly. 'I couldn't have let you marry Richard,' he told her forcefully. 'I seriously think your life could have been in danger if you had married him. I know you don't believe me at the moment, but soon I hope to be able to give you proof.' He leaned over, and dropped a light kiss on her forehead. 'I might be gone for a couple of hours,' he said. 'But don't worry—everything's going to be all right.'

As he went out, he turned on the television, and then closed and locked the door carefully behind him. She lay on the bed, listening to the sounds from below as he drove the horse-box out of the garage and closed the doors, and then drove away, the engine fading into the distance until she could hear no more.

What had he meant by those last words? Surely he couldn't seriously be accusing Richard of planning to hurt her? Richard loved her... And yet... Those dark eyes had been so compelling. For the first time she allowed herself to consider the possibility that he might be telling the truth...

The sheer vastness of the implications made her blink. What if it had been *Richard* all the time, Richard who had committed those burglaries, and framed Adam for them—Richard who wanted to marry her solely in order to ensure absolute control of the company?

Could she have been so deceived by him? It seemed impossible, and yet... Six years ago she had been prepared to believe that she had been deceived by Adam. Could Richard have been playing a very careful, very patient game all this time? Even making her believe that he wasn't sure about Adam's guilt, allowing her to convince herself...

Her brain was spinning in a whirlpool of confusion. Once she had begun to examine the seemingly outrageous proposition that Richard was the guilty party, it began to cast a very different light on everything that had happened. Of course, Richard would have had as little financial motive for committing those burglaries as Adam; but it was possible that his motivation could have had something to do with needing an outlet for his drive and intelligence that was denied him because of the way Lex had excluded him from real power in the company, in favour of Adam.

And Adam was right about one thing—for Richard, the company *was* an obsession. He could see success in no other terms. Maybe he had begun to plot a long time ago to remove Adam from his path. And then, with the sudden prospect of a marriage that would have given Adam an unassailable position, it had perhaps become urgent to him to do something drastic.

And, once Adam was safely out of the way, he could begin to court her himself, in his own fashion—knowing that he couldn't hope to compete with Adam in sweeping her off her feet, and playing instead on being the strong, dependable one, at a time when her whole world was in chaos.

Little things began to creep into her mind. That very first day, at the funeral, why had he used the word 'revenge'? She had attached little significance to it at the time—she had been so agitated at Adam's unexpected appearance that she had simply accepted his explanation. But it was a strange word for him to have chosen—unless it had slipped from his subconscious mind, unintentionally betraying the truth ...

But how *could* he have framed Adam? The crucial evidence had been about his car. Adam had said that on returning from the squash club he had put the car in his garage, locked it, and gone through to his house. There was absolutely no evidence that the garage had been broken into, or the car tampered with. And yet a witness had reported seeing it fifty miles away in Market Drayton, correctly recalling part of the number-plate, and the tyre-print had been found in a patch of soft ground close to the house that had been burgled.

Of course, it could have been another car of the same make and model, with false number-plates identical to Adam's— except for those tyre-prints. Unless ... The thought struck her so sharply that she jerked upright, forgetting that she was still tied up.

Tyres could be changed. What if Richard had hired a car, falsifying the number-plates, and, after carefully ensuring that a clear print had been left behind as evidence, he had *removed* the tyres from the hire car, and later put them on to Adam's car? It was so incredibly simple that it took her breath away. It could have been done...

But, on the other hand, she reminded herself with timely caution, just because it *could* have been done, it didn't necessarily follow that it *had* been done. She must be very careful about jumping to conclusions—it would be fatally easy to let her head follow her heart.

Experimentally she eased her wrists in her bonds. He had tied her very firmly—though not so tightly that it actually hurt. But she was going to have to resign herself to staying here until he should choose to return and release her. Fortunately the bed was comfortable. There was an old black and white film on the television, a light romantic comedy starring Cary Grant, and she settled down to watch it; at least she would have some distraction to pass the time.

It really was quite ludicrous, she reminded herself with a touch of wry humour. Here she was, trussed up like a Christmas turkey, calmly watching television when she was supposed to be getting married. The hunt for her must be well under way by now. What was Adam doing? Who owned this property? And how could he be so confident that they wouldn't be found here?

The film ended, and the news came on, first the national news, and then the local news. And there, slightly blurred on the screen, was her own face. It was an old photograph, and for a moment her only foolish thought was that she wished they had picked a better one. And there was Richard, looking distraught, flanked by detectives as he struggled bravely to answer the media's questions.

She watched him with a new cool objectivity. It seemed real enough, his concern—but what lay behind it? Was he genuinely afraid for the safety of the woman he loved—or was he worried that she might find out that all was not what it had seemed for these past six years?

It was some time before Adam returned—it was almost dark outside. She heard his footsteps, heard the key in the lock, and watched him covertly from beneath her lashes as he came in. There was nothing in his face to give away what he was thinking. How could he be so confident, so sure that nothing was going to go wrong?

He came over to the bed, and smiled down at her in teasing sympathy. 'I'm sorry to have left you for so long,' he said. 'Did you miss me?'

She gave him nothing, her eyes conveying only glittering resentment.

He laughed, and flicked on the light beside the bed, and then strolled over to close the curtains. 'You've been on the news, you know. Did you see it? "The Kidnapped Bride". Very touching. Ricky played his role to perfection, of course, but then he's had plenty of practice.'

He came back to sit on the side of the bed. 'I don't blame you for being taken in by him,' he murmured, smiling that smile she had always found so hard to resist. 'After all, everyone else was— even me, for a long while. And you were so very young then, so naïve. I should never have left you to his machinations when I went off to Australia—

I should have come back for you, made you listen to me. I should have made you come away with me then.'

She looked up at him, searching his eyes for some clue to what lay in his mind. But all she could see, in the soft glow of the bedside lamp, was that dark gleam that once she had thought was love. But how could she know? There were so many questions to be answered.

He laughed softly, and reached out to unfasten the gag around her mouth. It was a relief to have it off, and she drew a deep breath, shaking her hair loose. But her eyes were still suspicious as she slanted him a measured gaze. 'Why are you so sure that it was Richard who plotted against you?' she asked. 'I thought you used to be friends.'

He hesitated, a cloud of sadness in his eyes. 'We were, once—at least, I thought so,' he said. 'We'd grown up together—I thought of him as a brother. Maybe I attached too much importance to it, because I was an only child.'

She could tell that it was a subject he didn't want to talk about, but some feminine intuition told her that it wasn't because he was trying to make something up—it was more that it was a bad memory for him. 'What happened when you went up to university?' she persisted. 'Why did you quarrel?'

'He stole my project. It was the first piece of work we had to produce—it didn't even count towards the degree. But it was important in itself. Of course I never bothered to keep secret from him what I was working on—I discussed it with him quite freely, showed him my calculations. When I found out what he'd done, I just couldn't believe it. And the worst thing was the barefaced way he denied it—he insisted that it had been his idea in the first instance, and that I had cribbed it from *him*.'

His voice had a ring of absolute sincerity, and Olivia felt herself beginning to believe him. 'Why did you come back?' she asked, her voice unsteady.

'I told you,' he said. 'For Lex's funeral. I was very fond of him, you know, in a funny sort of way. And to settle up the loose ends with the company—perhaps to sell out my shares to you two, if that was what you wanted. I only intended to stay for a week or two.'

'So why did you stay?'

He smiled grimly. 'Partly because I began to hear a lot of bad things about the way Richard was running things. The take-over bids, the asset stripping—I didn't like it, and I didn't feel I could just walk away as if it was nothing to do with me. He was doing the dirty on people who were old friends of mine—Mike Sauter, for one. I couldn't let him get away with that.'

'You went to a great deal of trouble to stop him.' She was close to letting herself be convinced, but still some suspicions lurked.

He nodded assent. 'The more I found out about what was going on, the more determined I was,' he said. 'And then as I began to realise what a devious bastard he could be, I began to put two and two together. I'd known *someone* had framed me six years ago, but I had no idea who it could be. It never even occurred to me that it could have been Richard—I never knew he hated me that much.'

His dark eyes gazed down into hers, and she felt herself drowning in their depths. 'He cheated us both, Angel,' he murmured, his low, husky voice caressing her. 'He cheated us of six long years. Let's not cheat ourselves of any more.'

She hesitated, her heart longing to surrender. But still nagging voices whispered in her mind. 'I . . . I don't know,' she prevaricated, struggling to fight that mesmerising power that was in danger of swaying her judgement. 'You said that you could show me proof that you were innocent.'

'I could show you things that might help convince you. But if you can't trust me until I give you proof, how will either of us ever feel sure that you can trust me enough? Try following your instincts.' He stroked his hand down over her cheek, lifting her chin so that she had to look up at him. 'Trust me tonight, Angel—without proof,' he pleaded, soft and sincere. 'Show me that you love me.'

And as she gazed up into his eyes she knew that her heart could give only one answer. 'Yes,' she whispered, her love for him spilling over. 'I trust you.'

CHAPTER NINE

ADAM'S mouth came down on hers in a kiss that began lightly, but flamed swiftly into a scorching heat as his plundering tongue swept deep into the sweetest corners of her mouth, meeting no resistance at all. Her hands were still tied behind her back, but she didn't ask him to untie them. It was a measure of how much she trusted him that she should allow herself to be so totally defenceless.

He lifted his head to look down at her, smiling slowly as he surveyed her virginal white dress. 'I think,' he murmured, his voice smoky from the fires blazing in his eyes, 'the first thing must be to do something about this.'

'It'll take you quite a while,' she cautioned him teasingly. 'There's about a hundred buttons.'

He smiled in warming anticipation. 'Then I'd better get started.'

He worked slowly, unfastening each of the tiny pearl buttons down her back one by one, his eyes telling her that he was enjoying this task more than any other he had ever undertaken in his life. She gazed up at him shyly, remembering that other time, six years ago, when they had lain on the grassy banks of the stream, and he had taken off her bikini top. But this time, she knew, he wasn't going to stop or push her away. She had taken a one-way ticket, and she was going all the way.

But still there were a few womanly uncertainties troubling her mind. 'What about Joanna Marston?' she asked, a tinge of jealousy in her voice.

He laughed softly, shaking his head. 'I took her out to dinner once.'

'And Georgina?' she persisted, knowing that that connection could not be so easily passed over.

'What about Georgina?'

'Wasn't there...something between you once?' she questioned, not at all sure that she really wanted to know.

He paused in unfastening her dress, and looked her straight in the eye. 'Yes, there was,' he conceded frankly. 'A very long time ago. But then she got married, and that was the end of it.'

She lifted one enquiring eyebrow—she had to be sure that he was telling the truth. 'The absolute end? You didn't keep seeing her after she was married?'

A dark frown crossed his face. 'No, I didn't,' he insisted forcefully. 'Don't you know I wouldn't do a thing like that?'

She nodded quickly. 'I know,' she whispered, afraid that she had made him angry. 'It was just that Richard said——'

'Richard!' He snorted in scorn. 'He told you I was having an affair with Georgie after she was married?'

'Well, not in so many words,' she admitted fairly. 'He just sort of implied it. He let me think that was the reason you'd quarrelled at university.'

'I told you the reason why we quarrelled.'

'Yes.' She offered him a tremulous smile of apology, her eyes shyly inviting him to continue with what he had been doing.

He laughed softly. 'Oh, Angel—when you look at me like that...' His arms folded around her, wrapping her to him, and his mouth took hers, a little fierce as if to punish her for her doubt. His ravaging tongue plundered all the sweetest depths, igniting fires inside her, and her head tipped back as she surrendered all she had to his demanding embrace.

His hand had returned to continue unfastening her buttons, and even as the kiss ended she knew that she was safe enough to tease him a little. 'But you know, you can't blame me altogether for wondering about you and Georgie,' she argued, slanting him a mischievous look from beneath her lashes. 'After all, she's always seemed rather keen on you.' Her eyes danced at the deliberate understatement.

He smiled wryly. 'That became a bit of a turn-off after a while,' he remarked. 'Poor Georgie—I'm afraid she was rather spoiled when she was young, and grew up to think she could always have whatever she wanted. She thought I was going to marry her. I suppose at twenty she was ready for marriage, but I was only eighteen and I certainly wasn't—and I made that quite clear. So she thought she could make me jealous by marrying someone else. When that didn't work either, she seemed to become embittered and hard. I don't like to think that the way she is today could have been partly my fault.'

She rested her head against his shoulder, her heart touched by the shadow of guilt in his eyes. 'How was it you came to Lex's funeral with her?' she asked.

'I didn't. We met quite by chance outside the church—we were both a little late—and I fell in with her out of old friendship. I suppose I'd been a little uncertain of the sort of reception I was going to get, and it felt better with at least one supporter by my side. Unfortunately she hadn't learnt a great deal more subtlety with maturing years—her invitation after the funeral was . . . a little embarrassing on both sides.'

She flashed him a look of mock anger. 'It wasn't very nice of you to try and taunt me with it,' she scolded.

'Ah . . .' He had undone enough buttons now to be able to slip her dress down over her slim shoulders. 'But I wanted to make you jealous.'

Her mouth was dry with anticipation as she felt him run his fingers along the top edge of the silk, easing the bodice down a fraction lower. Beneath the tightly structured whalebone she hadn't needed to wear a bra, and her breasts were bare—as he was going to find out any second. 'You . . . almost succeeded,' she managed rather breathlessly, struggling to maintain her side of this inconsequential conversation.

'Did I?' He seemed totally fascinated by the smooth texture of her skin as slowly—oh, so agonisingly slowly—he uncovered a little more of her naked breasts. 'Aren't you going to ask me why else I decided to stay?'

'It . . . wasn't just to do with the company, then?'

He shook his head, his eyes remaining fixed on the smooth, firm swell he was slowly revealing.

'Then what was it?'

Just a fraction more uncovered one taut, pink nipple, pertly inviting, and his smooth hand stroked beneath her breast, lifting it clear of the silk, as if that was his answer. 'I thought I'd managed to forget you, Angel,' he murmured, his eyes dark as fire as they gazed down into hers. 'Even when I saw in the papers that you'd got engaged to Richard, I hardly lost any sleep. But when I saw you again I knew I still wanted you as much as ever.'

His thumb brushed lightly over the tender rosebud peak, sending a warm shimmer of response through her. 'Seeing you in the flesh, I knew that no bitterness I might have felt when you turned against me could stop me loving you. And when I saw you with Richard, so cool, so bloodless, I knew you didn't really love him. You *couldn't* love him — you aren't made for that sort of anaemic relationship.'

The incredible things his clever fingers were doing suggested the proof of that. She moaned softly, her body arching towards him as he eased the bodice of her dress further down, baring both ripe, succulent breasts to his expert caresses. He laughed, low in his throat, savouring every naked curve with the eyes of a hungry man.

'When you were seventeen, I fell in love with your sweetness and your innocence,' he went on, his voice a husky counterpoint to his lingering touch. 'I'd watched you grow from a child to a young woman, and I had a feeling my heart was going to be in danger.

'What took me by surprise was how suddenly it happened. There you were one day, so beautiful you almost took my breath away, and every time I looked at you you'd blush. I was almost shocked at the thoughts I was having. I told myself you were far too young, and that I ought to back off, wait a little while until you were older. But I couldn't keep away from you . . .'

His voice trailed away on a sensuous growl, and he bent his head to lap at one deliciously sensitive nipple with his hot, rasping tongue. She gazed down at his dark head, bent over her breast, with a kind of incredulous wonder. So often she had dreamed of him making love to her like this, but none of her dreams had ever——

And then as he took the sweet, tender bud into his mouth, and began to suckle with a deep, pulsing rhythm, all conscious thought evaporated. She was all sensation, her whole body awash with response, her spine curling in ecstasy as she strained against the soft bonds that held her wrists. She was his prisoner, his to do with whatever he wished, but she never, ever wanted him to stop.

She was barely even aware that he had lifted the hem of her skirt, brushing it back over the smooth length of her thighs, until she felt the caressing touch of his hand on those few inches of satin skin above the tops of her white silk stockings. She opened her eyes, looking up at him in trusting shyness as he gazed down at her possessively.

'You always were mine, from the very beginning,' he murmured. 'The fates have watched over you, and kept you for me, even when I was trying to forget you.'

He knelt over her, and with slow deliberation he unfastened first one pair, then the other, of her suspenders. Savouring every inch of her long legs, he rolled down her stockings, pausing only to unfasten the silk scarf around her ankles. She lay watching him, vulnerable and submissive; now only a pair of dainty white lace briefs protected her innocence.

'Mine. And now I'm going to have what I waited for.' He laughed, a low, sensuous growl, and, grasping the delicate scrap of lace, he stripped it down, tossing it somewhere on the floor.

She gazed up at him, suddenly a little apprehensive. Those dark, mesmerising eyes held hers, compelling her into surrender as he slid his hand up smoothly between her slender thighs, parting them insistently. The trembling uncertainty as she recognised his intent gave way to a moan of sheer ecstasy as she felt the gentle touch of his fingers, seeking the most intimate caresses. A sweet sensation, like melting honey, flowed through her body, and she parted her thighs for him willingly, inviting any liberty he cared to take.

He had the exquisite skill of an expert, shocking her slightly, arousing her more with every move he made. He had unfolded the moist velvet petals, finding the secret seed-pearl hidden beneath them, and a wild quiver of response ran through her as she abandoned herself totally to this world of sheer carnal gratification he was leading her into.

He was making an erotic feast of her body, tasting every inch of her skin with his hot mouth, and she lay helplessly responsive beneath his possessive caresses. Even her toes didn't escape his attention—she shrieked and wriggled as he nibbled at them with his strong white teeth, pretending that she was trying to escape.

But there was no possibility of escape. Her hands were still tied, and she had no breath to beg him to untie them, even if she had wanted to. And as he cradled her in his arms, his breath warm against her cheek, his heart thundering with a powerful rhythm, she knew that he had forgotten.

'I couldn't keep away from you, Angel,' he murmured, nuzzling into her hair, his soft voice part of the hypnotic spell he was weaving around her as he continued to caress her with slow, sensuous possessiveness. 'I still felt you were too young, but then after all my mother was barely eighteen when she married my father, and they were the happiest couple I ever knew. And I began to think how easily life, and all the things we take so much for granted when we're young, could be snatched away, and I thought . . . why take the risk of waiting? Why not grab at happiness with both hands while we had the chance?'

There was a wistful note in his voice, and she gazed up at him, knowing just what he was thinking. It *had* all been snatched away—he had lost everything, found himself in prison . . . an innocent man. Her heart twisted in pain for him,

and one single tear escaped from the corner of her
eye and tracked down her cheek.

He smiled down at her, and brushed the tear away
with a gentle hand. 'No, don't cry, Angel,' he whispered. 'The time for crying's over. From now on,
there'll only be love.' He moved to lie above her,
his thighs coaxing hers further apart. 'Don't be
frightened,' he soothed. 'I won't hurt you.'

He kissed the corners of her eyes, and then his
mouth closed over hers, his sensuous tongue
swirling deep inside, seeking out every sensitive
corner. And she felt only a sweet tide of feminine
submissiveness flow through her as with one
smooth, easy thrust he took her, causing not even
a shred of pain.

For a long moment he held still, letting them both
savour the deep satisfaction of knowing that at last
their love had won. And then he began to move,
slowly at first, the thick muscles in his shoulders
clenching as he held his weight from crushing her.
And some ancient instinct, as old as Eve, taught
her to move with him, inviting the deepest measure
of his demand.

With a small grunt of surprise he realised that
her wrists were still tied behind her back, and deftly
he unfastened them, freeing her to wrap her arms
tightly around him, to hold him to her, to feel the
sweat-slicked smoothness of his powerful muscles
beneath her hands.

They broke the rhythm just long enough to allow
him to lift her dress off over her head, tossing it
aside, and she only knew that he had removed his
own clothes when she felt the rough hairs that scat-

tered his hard chest rasp against her tender breasts. She let her fingertips trail down the length of his spine, delighted by the tremor that ran through him, telling her that she was giving him as much pleasure as he was giving her.

Their naked bodies entwined, exchanging heat, fusing in a pulsing furnace, melting them both as the fierce ache in the pit of her stomach began to grow and spread outwards, flooding through her whole body, and as he forgot to be gentle they rode together right into the heart of the fire, beating at the flames that lifted them higher and higher until they seemed to be spinning somewhere in the outer regions of space.

And then with a last wild cry she seemed to tip over the edge of some vast precipice, and felt herself falling, falling, as they tumbled together on the bed, exhausted and replete; and he collapsed into her arms, all the strength drained from his powerful body, and she stroked his hair, her heart brimming over with love.

She woke to the smell of fresh coffee being brewed, and stretched lazily in the bed, her body still aching comfortably from their night of lovemaking. If they had wasted six years, they had certainly done their best to make up for it last night, she reflected, a tinge of pink colouring her cheeks at the memory.

He had produced a Chinese meal he had bought from a take-away, and a bottle of champagne, and they had feasted in bed, and he had let the cool sparkling wine trickle down over her body so that he could lick it away, making her gurgle with laughter.

She sat up. Her wedding dress was lying in a crumpled heap on the floor, the white silk now sullied by a few grubby marks. She eyed it with wry irony. She had certainly had a wedding-night—though without benefit of clergy, and with the wrong man.

But then Adam turned from the kitchenette, and smiled at her, and she corrected herself quickly. It had been the right man—so very right. Naked, she slipped out of bed, and walked into his arms, lifting her face for his kiss.

The rasp of his clothes against her soft bare skin was delicious. He kissed her long and tenderly, curving her hard against him, smoothing his hand down the length of her spine in a possessive gesture that hinted that the pleasures of the night were far from exhausted.

'Mmm—what a nice way to say good morning,' he murmured appreciatively.

She gurgled with laughter. 'But what am I going to put on?' she asked. 'I can't put that on again.' She nodded her head towards her discarded dress.

He held her at arm's length, his dark gaze surveying her naked body with evident delight. 'You'll just have to stay like that all day,' he teased. 'What a lovely thought!'

Her eyes danced. He made her feel so exquisitely feminine and desirable; she would have happily stayed here all day—all year, all of her life—making love with him. But there were still some issues unresolved. 'What about the police?' she asked apprehensively. 'Shouldn't we let them know they can call off their search? And then there's Richard.'

'Ah, yes—Richard. He should be here soon—I laid a little treasure-trail for him to follow. We'd better go over to the house and wait for him. So I'm afraid I'll have to let you get dressed after all,' he conceded reluctantly. 'There are some clothes for you in that bag over there.'

He indicated a canvas hold-all in the corner. She went over and peeped inside. There were jeans, and an embroidered smock-top of softest cotton lawn— the sort of things she used to wear six years ago, but very far from her image of recent times. She turned her head to slant him a quizzical smile. 'You do realise I'm not seventeen any more?' she teased.

He came over and wrapped his arms around her from behind, burying his face in her hair. 'To me, you'll always be seventeen. Even when we're both old and fat, with grey hair and great-grandchildren, I'll still look at you and see a laughing teenager on a riverbank,' he vowed, the husky sincerity of his voice making a promise that would stand for sixty years.

She had guessed that their hiding-place had been the chauffeur's quarters of some large house—but she hadn't guessed *which* house. 'My goodness,' she breathed as they walked hand-in-hand across the wide sweep of gravel drive to the front door. 'Weren't you afraid that this would be the first place they'd look?'

He shook his head. 'No one knows that I've bought it back yet. It was never even on the market—I approached the owners direct, and they agreed to sell. In fact it was probably the last place anyone would have thought of looking,' he added with that slow smile that could make him look, if you didn't know him better, like the devil himself.

It was the house his parents had owned, the house he had grown up in. Of mellowed red-brown brick, it rambled without any apparent plan, the ivy and wistaria that covered its walls blurring the distinction between it and the colourful garden that surrounded it.

'I'm glad it's still exactly the same as it used to be,' she said, squeezing his hand. 'It's such a lovely house.'

He smiled down at her. 'Perhaps I should carry you over the threshold?' he suggested teasingly. 'I know we're not actually married yet, but that's just a technicality.'

She slanted him a glowing look from beneath her lashes. 'Oh, I think you should,' she agreed, mock-seriously. 'After all, even though we're doing it all backwards, we shouldn't miss anything out.'

He laughed, and scooped her up in his strong arms, and strode with her up the steps to the front door. He paused to insert his key, and then they were inside the hall. The house was as charming inside as it was out, filled with light and flowers, the furniture and floors gleaming with generations of beeswax.

'Welcome to your new home, Mrs Taylor-to-be,' he announced, setting her on her feet.

'Oh... It's beautiful!' she breathed, her heart soaring in happiness. 'Will you show me all round?'

'Of course. I'm not properly settled in yet. Some of the rooms aren't furnished—we can do that together. But quite a bit of my parents' stuff is still here. Come and see.'

It brought back so many memories, strolling round the old house together. In the main bedroom she could almost smell the perfume of white roses that Aunt Lizzie had always used to wear. And the drawing-room was just as she remembered it, looking out over a paved terrace and a small pond fringed with reeds.

Six years ago she had been dreaming of coming here as a bride—but then Adam had been sent to prison, and the house had been sold to strangers. Well, she was here now, she wanted to tell the quiet building—just a few years late.

They ended their tour in a side room downstairs—a room that now Adam had taken over as an office. The banks of sophisticated computers and communications equipment were impressive, to say the least. Olivia looked up at him, bewildered.

'What's all this?'

'This, my little love, is what I promised to show you. The fruits of five years of my labours—and with not one penny of LTS money.' He sat down, drawing her on to his lap, and turned on one of the screens. A spread-sheet appeared, details of company accounts. 'My companies. Why did it never occur to you that I might be doing something other than wasting my days as the playboy of the southern hemisphere?'

'I . . . I don't know.' The evidence was before her eyes. Adam had moved very far beyond the realms of a small private company like Lambert, Taylor & Simpson. So much for Richard's small-minded insistence that he was plotting some Machiavellian scheme to regain his old power—he had power in abundance through this international business empire he had created. She gazed at the computer screens, amazed by the vast span of his enterprises. He certainly hadn't spent the past five years living the life of a playboy! 'You set up all this with what you inherited from your mother?' she asked.

He nodded. 'I'd already bought into a few firms in Australia,' he said. 'When I came out of prison, it seemed the logical place to go—as far away from Derbyshire as I could get. And financially it was a very good move—business is booming down there, with the economies of the Pacific Rim right on the doorstep. I could hardly go wrong.'

She smiled wryly—such modesty couldn't disguise the talent and sheer hard work that must have gone into it all. 'If you didn't use any of the dividends from LTS, what did you do with them?' she asked curiously.

'They were all covenanted to a charity that looks after ex-prisoners. It runs workshops for them, to help them learn skills so they can get jobs.'

'*What?* Oh, Richard will be furious when he finds that out!' She gurgled with laughter. 'He didn't even want me to send anything to the Ethiopian Famine Relief—he said they should take care of their own problems!' Slipping off his lap, she wandered around the room, examining the equipment.

'You're going to run everything from here?' she asked.

'Mostly. I'll still need to travel a little, but I've put very efficient chief executives into all my operations, and I'll be leaving the day-to-day running to them. I'd always planned to come back to England some time—what's happened has just speeded things up a little.'

'Are you going to take over LTS?' she asked.

'If Richard can be persuaded to sell.'

'He won't want to,' she mused. 'He could never see beyond LTS—"The Company", he always calls it, with capital letters. From the way he speaks, you'd think it was the only company in the world.'

He smiled wryly. 'That was the one thing he learned from Lex. He could never imagine carving out anything for himself—he only ever wanted to step into Lex's shoes.' He spoke almost as if he pitied him, and Olivia gazed up at him in surprise. After all the harm he had done, he could still forgive him?

'What will you do about him?' she asked. 'Do you have enough evidence to prove to the police what he did?'

'No—and I don't know if I ever will. Harry's trying to find out for me if there are any whispers on the underworld grapevine—who he associates with, whether he's been involved in anything illegal since the art thefts.'

Olivia shivered. 'He scared me, that man,' she confided. 'How come you're so friendly with him?'

He smiled down at her. 'You shouldn't judge by appearances,' he chided gently. 'Harry's no criminal—he's an honest businessman. He's made most of his money in scrap metal, but he likes racing so he owns a couple of race-horses, and he likes a game of cards so he bought himself a club—it's more or less a toy to him.'

She looked up at him questioningly. 'What was he in prison for, then?' she asked.

'He'd been accused of a massive tax fraud—but in fact it was a crooked accountant who was responsible. What Harry didn't like people to know was that he couldn't read. He'd made all that money—he's worth a cool couple of million—without ever having been to school. So I taught him—and then he was able to work out what his accountant had done. He appealed with the new evidence, and his conviction was quashed. And we've remained good friends ever since.'

'Why didn't you tell me that at the time?' she appealed, feeling more than a little ashamed of herself.

'Because, my little love, you were being so obstinate in your prejudice, I thought it was highly likely that you'd simply refuse to believe me,' He swung her up in the air, letting her fall down into his arms. 'I hope you've learned your lesson.'

'Oh, yes.' She swept him a humbly chastened look, calculated to make him laugh. 'I'm sorry.'

His head bent towards hers. 'So you should be——'

'Well, well. What a cosy little scene.'

A voice of cutting sarcasm, sharp as a whiplash, broke them abruptly apart. Olivia looked up sharply, and caught her breath in shock. 'Richard! What——?'

'What am I doing here?' He moved into the room, his eyes surveying her with cold contempt. 'I've come to finish what I started six years ago. And I find you both here together—how very convenient. I couldn't have arranged it better if I'd planned it myself.'

He put his hand into the inside pocket of his jacket, and as she stared in disbelief he produced a small, lethal-looking gun. Chilling fingers of fear curled around her heart; she had absolutely no doubt that it was his intention to kill them both.

Adam was very still, but she could feel the tension in him. 'What's the point of killing us?' he asked, his level voice coolly defying the threat. 'I'm prepared to buy out your share of LTS. You can take the money and go anywhere you like, a free man and a wealthy one. If you kill us, you'll spend the rest of your life in prison—and that's not a pleasant prospect, believe me.'

Richard smiled with a kind of twisted humour. 'Oh, I've no intention of going to prison,' he asserted with confidence. 'It's such a tragic story. I discovered you were hiding out here, you see, and came rushing over at once—too desperate to rescue my poor bride to wait for the police. And when I got here I found that you'd raped and murdered her—strangled, I think, don't you? And then you attacked me with a gun—this one—but I managed to wrest it from you, and in the struggle I shot you in self-defence. Oh, no, I won't go to prison.'

Olivia stared at him in amazement. He really thought he could get away with it—the sheer cold calculation of it almost took her breath away. 'It's too late,' she blurted out in desperation.

Richard's eyes flickered to her in mild astonishment, and he lifted his eyebrows. 'Oh?'

'We know it was you who framed Adam, and we know how you did it,' she asserted wildly. 'You hired a car like Adam's, and did the burglary, and then you swapped the tyres on to his car so the tyre-print would match.'

Just for a second, there was a waver of uncertainty in Richard's eyes. She felt Adam give her a swift squeeze of congratulation, and at once he picked up on what she had said. 'That's right, Ricky. And my investigators have traced the car-hire company's records.'

But Richard was swift to regain his confidence. 'You're bluffing,' he sneered. 'They won't have kept the records for six years.'

'How much do you want to stake on that?' Adam challenged with dry amusement. 'Your freedom for the rest of your life?'

Richard looked confused. He tried a mocking smile, as if to deny that he had lost the initiative. But he couldn't be sure—there was too much at stake.

'So why don't we discuss my original offer?' suggested Adam cordially. 'I'm prepared to buy out your share of LTS—for cash. And you'd better hope that we both remain in good health for a very long time, because if anything happens to either of us the evidence we have will go straight to the hands of the police, and no imaginative little story you might dream up will get you off the hook.'

Richard hesitated, and then sat down heavily. 'Damn you, Taylor,' he snarled, laying aside his gun. 'Damn you.'

EPILOGUE

THE leather executive chair behind the chairman's desk was large, but it was comfortable. Olivia had a feeling she could get used to it—but of course once Adam got back from Australia this would be his office. A wistful little sigh escaped her lips. She was longing to have him back, of course, but...she would miss the satisfaction of running the company, even though she had only been in charge for three weeks.

Idly she twirled the plain gold wedding band that he had placed on her finger, next to the sapphire and diamond engagement ring he had put there so long ago. The wedding had been such a rush—by special licence—but incredibly Mrs James had still had the wedding dress she had made for her when she was seventeen, and it had still been a perfect fit. And, though there had been only a few guests, it had been a lovely wedding.

Her glance strayed to the portrait of Lex, frowning down from the wall. What would he have thought of everything that had happened? He would probably have insisted that he had known all along that Adam was innocent, she reflected with a smile of wry reminiscence. He had never had much trouble convincing himself of his own omniscience. Well, finally his plans had come to fruition—Adam was at last chairman of LTS...

She looked up quickly as the door opened, and every other thought evaporated as Adam appeared. With a cry of joy she threw herself across the room, and into his arms. 'Adam! Oh...' Anything else she might have been going to say was silenced by his kiss.

He lifted her in his arms, and carried her over to the desk, sitting down in the big chair and settling her in his lap. She nestled against him, breathing with a happy sigh the familiar musky scent of his body. 'I didn't think you'd be back today. I wasn't expecting you until tomorrow, at least.'

'I came home a day early. And I drove all the way from Heathrow at a speed that would have had every traffic cop in the country on my tail if they'd spotted me. I couldn't wait to get back to you.'

She closed her eyes, luxuriating in the sheer pleasure of having him here. He had had to go away so soon after their wedding, to sort out the transfer of his business affairs to England, and she had had to stay behind and run the company in his absence.

'You won't have to go back to Australia for a while now, will you?' she asked, seeking reassurance.

'No. Just the occasional trip—and you'll be coming with me. I don't want to be separated from you again.' His arms wrapped around her possessively, holding her close. 'I can't forget how close I let us come to disaster that day. I nearly underestimated Richard once too often. If it hadn't been for your cool thinking...'

She gurgled with laughter, snuggling up against him. 'You were pretty cool too,' she reminded him. 'Poor Richard—I can't help feeling a little bit sorry for him, wasting all those years in bitterness and envy.'

'Well, we don't have to worry about him any more,' he assured her. 'I've got enough dirt on his business dealings to keep the Serious Fraud Squad and the Inland Revenue sniffing around for years. He'll hardly dare to breathe without clearing it with me first.'

'Good.' She smiled up at him, still wondering at the twists and turns of fate that had snatched him away from her, and now had brought him back. One thing at least was certain—they would never take their happiness for granted.

'So how have things been while I've been away?' he asked. 'No problems?'

'Nothing serious.' In truth, there had been a number of problems generated by Richard's abrupt departure, but she had enjoyed dealing with them, and was pleased with her success. 'I suppose...now that you're back, you'll be taking over,' she added diffidently.

He slanted her a look of surprise. 'No. I told you, I put a good chief executive in charge of all my companies, and let them run themselves.'

'Oh...' Surely he couldn't be planning to bring in a stranger? 'So who do you have in mind?' she asked, ready to challenge him.

He laughed in teasing mockery. 'Oh, I don't think I'll have to look very far.' His eyes told her exactly who he meant. 'In fact, I might consider inter-

viewing the only possible candidate right now.'
Except that the things he was doing with his hand
were reducing that candidate to a state of helpless
giggles.

'You mean it?' she demanded, trying to catch
her breath. 'You really think I can handle it?'

'Of course—who better? You know the company
inside out, the customers trust you, the workforce
trusts you...' His voice was quite matter-of-fact,
even though he was deftly unfastening the buttons
down the front of her businesslike silk shirt.

'Well...before I accept,' she announced, her
voice serious but her eyes dancing, 'I'd like to
discuss the matter of a contract.'

'A contract?' His gaze was completely fascinated
by the sight of her ripe, warm breasts, half hidden
in the delicate lacy cups of her bra.

'Uh-huh. To include a clause about maternity
leave.'

His eyes flew to her face. 'Maternity leave?' His
smile hovered between hope and delight. 'And—
er—how soon do you anticipate that you might be
requiring maternity leave, Mrs Taylor?'

She tipped her head on one side, playfully re-
arranging his tie. 'Oh, I think...maybe quite soon.'

HARLEQUIN ◆ PRESENTS®

Dark secrets...
forbidden desires...
scandalous discoveries...
an enthralling six-part saga from a bright new talent!

HEARTS OF FIRE
by Miranda Lee

This exciting new family saga is set in the glamorous world
of opal dealing in Australia. *HEARTS OF FIRE* unfolds over
six books, revealing the passion, scandal, sin and hope that
exist between two fabulously rich families. Each novel
features its own gripping romance—but you'll also be
hooked by the continuing story of Gemma Smith's search
for the truth about her real mother, and the priceless
Black Opal. And her fight for the love of ruthless seducer
Nathan Whitmore...

Coming next month

Book 1: *Seduction & Sacrifice* by Miranda Lee

Everyone warned Gemma about Nathan, but she believed he
wasn't heartless—just heartbroken! Clearly, he was still in
love with his ex-wife, Lenore, so Gemma knew she must hide
her overwhelming attraction to him....

Harlequin Presents #1754: you'll want to know what
happens next!

Available in July wherever Harlequin books are sold.

HARLEQUIN PRESENTS®

Don't be late for the wedding!

Be sure to make a date for the happy event—

The first in our tantalizing new selection of stories...

Wedlocked!
Bonded in matrimony, torn by desire...

Next month, watch for:
A Bride for the Taking by Sandra Marton
Harlequin Presents #1751

Dorian had a problem, and there was only one solution: she
had to become Jake Prince's wife! Jake was all too willing to
make love to her, but they both knew their marriage was a
sham. The trouble was, Dorian soon realized she wanted
more, much more, than a few nights of bliss in his arms and
a pretense of love—she wanted that pretense to
become reality....

Available in July wherever Harlequin books are sold.

HARLEQUIN PRESENTS®

Ever felt the excitement of a dangerous desire...?

The thrill of a feverish flirtation...?

Passion is guaranteed with our new selection of sensual stories.

Indulge in...

Dangerous Liaisons
Falling in love is a risky affair!

Coming next month:

Tainted Love by Alison Fraser

Harlequin Presents #1753

Clare Anderson was a prisoner of passion, a woman with a past...and Fen Marchand clearly didn't have a high opinion of her! But he was father to ten-year-old Miles and badly in need of a housekeeper...so badly in need that he agreed to take on Clare. The physical attraction between them was powerful—but unwanted! Clare had to keep her distance. Fen must never know that the risks she'd taken had been for the sake of her precious son....

Available in July wherever Harlequin books are sold.

ANNOUNCING THE

PRIZE SURPRISE SWEEPSTAKES!

This month's prize:

L-A-R-G-E—SCREEN PANASONIC TV!

This month, as a special surprise, we're giving away a fabulous FREE TV!

Imagine how delighted you and your family will be to own this brand-new 31" Panasonic** television! It comes with all the latest high-tech features, like a SuperFlat picture tube for a clear, crisp picture...unified remote control...closed-caption decoder...clock and sleep timer, and much more!

The facing page contains two Entry Coupons (as does every book you received this shipment). Complete and return *all* the entry coupons; **the more times you enter, the better your chances of winning the TV!**

Then keep your fingers crossed, because you'll find out by July 15, 1995 if you're the winner!

Remember: The more times you enter, the better your chances of winning!*

*NO PURCHASE OR OBLIGATION TO CONTINUE BEING A SUBSCRIBER NECESSARY TO ENTER. SEE THE REVERSE SIDE OF ANY ENTRY COUPON FOR ALTERNATE MEANS OF ENTRY.

**THE PROPRIETORS OF THE TRADEMARK ARE NOT ASSOCIATED WITH THIS PROMOTION.

PTV KAL

PRIZE SURPRISE
SWEEPSTAKES
OFFICIAL ENTRY COUPON

This entry must be received by: JUNE 30, 1995
This month's winner will be notified by: JULY 15, 1995

YES, I want to win the Panasonic 31" TV! Please enter me in the drawing and let me know if I've won!

Name_____

Address _____ Apt. _____

| City | State/Prov. | Zip/Postal Code |

Account #_____

Return entry with invoice in reply envelope.

© 1995 HARLEQUIN ENTERPRISES LTD.   CTV KAL

PRIZE SURPRISE
SWEEPSTAKES
OFFICIAL ENTRY COUPON

This entry must be received by: JUNE 30, 1995
This month's winner will be notified by: JULY 15, 1995

YES, I want to win the Panasonic 31" TV! Please enter me in the drawing and let me know if I've won!

Name_____

Address _____ Apt. _____

| City | State/Prov. | Zip/Postal Code |

Account #_____

Return entry with invoice in reply envelope.

© 1995 HARLEQUIN ENTERPRISES LTD.   CTV KAL

OFFICIAL RULES

PRIZE SURPRISE SWEEPSTAKES 3448

NO PURCHASE OR OBLIGATION NECESSARY

Three Harlequin Reader Service 1995 shipments will contain respectively, coupons for entry into three different prize drawings, one for a Panasonic 31" wide-screen TV, another for a 5-piece Wedgwood china service for eight and the third for a Sharp ViewCam camcorder. To enter any drawing using an Entry Coupon, simply complete and mail according to directions.

There is no obligation to continue using the Reader Service to enter and be eligible for any prize drawing. You may also enter any drawing by hand printing the words "Prize Surprise," your name and address on a 3"x5" card and the name of the prize you wish that entry to be considered for (i.e., Panasonic wide-screen TV, Wedgwood china or Sharp ViewCam). Send your 3"x5" entries via first-class mail (limit: one per envelope) to: Prize Surprise Sweepstakes 3448, c/o the prize you wish that entry to be considered for, P.O. Box 1315, Buffalo, NY 14269-1315, USA or P.O. Box 610, Fort Erie, Ontario L2A 5X3, Canada.

To be eligible for the Panasonic wide-screen TV, entries must be received by 6/30/95; for the Wedgwood china, 8/30/95; and for the Sharp ViewCam, 10/30/95.

Winners will be determined in random drawings conducted under the supervision of D.L. Blair, Inc., an independent judging organization whose decisions are final, from among all eligible entries received for that drawing. Approximate prize values are as follows: Panasonic wide-screen TV ($1,800); Wedgwood china ($840) and Sharp ViewCam ($2,000). Sweepstakes open to residents of the U.S. (except Puerto Rico) and Canada, 18 years of age or older. Employees and immediate family members of Harlequin Enterprises, Ltd., D.L. Blair, Inc., their affiliates, subsidiaries and all other agencies, entities and persons connected with the use, marketing or conduct of this sweepstakes are not eligible. Odds of winning a prize are dependent upon the number of eligible entries received for that drawing. Prize drawing and winner notification for each drawing will occur no later than 15 days after deadline for entry eligibility for that drawing. Limit: one prize to an individual, family or organization. All applicable laws and regulations apply. Sweepstakes offer void wherever prohibited by law. Any litigation within the province of Quebec respecting the conduct and awarding of the prizes in this sweepstakes must be submitted to the Regies des loteries et Courses du Quebec. In order to win a prize, residents of Canada will be required to correctly answer a time-limited arithmetical skill-testing question. Value of prizes are in U.S. currency.

Winners will be obligated to sign and return an Affidavit of Eligibility within 30 days of notification. In the event of noncompliance within this time period, prize may not be awarded. If any prize or prize notification is returned as undeliverable, that prize will not be awarded. By acceptance of a prize, winner consents to use of his/her name, photograph or other likeness for purposes of advertising, trade and promotion on behalf of Harlequin Enterprises, Ltd., without further compensation, unless prohibited by law.

For the names of prizewinners (available after 12/31/95), send a self-addressed, stamped envelope to: Prize Surprise Sweepstakes 3448 Winners, P.O. Box 4200, Blair, NE 68009.

RPZ KAL